"I'M TOO OLD FOR YOU," HE TOLD HER ROUGHLY.

"Is that what all this is about? Your age?" She smiled tenderly and stepped closer, enveloping him in the delicate scent of her perfume. "Sean, what difference does it make? I love *you*, not some number that says how old you are."

He looked down into her earnest expression and wondered what he had ever done to deserve such torture. She was offering him heaven on a plate and he dared not accept. He closed his eyes against the temptation she represented and stepped away from her abruptly. He had to end this now or he'd never find the strength to leave her.

"Aren't you forgetting something?" He made his voice deliberately harsh. "There's more to be considered than just your feelings."

CANDLELIGHT ECSTASY ROMANCES

DESPERATE YEARNING

Dallas Hamlin

A CANDLELIGHT ECSTASY ROMANCE ®

Published by
Dell Publishing Co., Inc.
1 Dag Hammarskjold Plaza
New York, New York 10017

Dell ® TM 681510, Dell Publishing Co., Inc.
Candlelight Ecstasy Romance®, 1,203,540, is a registered
trademark of Dell Publishing Co., Inc.,
New York, New York.

ISBN: 0–440–11909–X

Printed in the United States of America
First printing—August 1984

*To my husband, Art, who never
complained about having a typewriter as
a dinner companion.
And to my mother, Kathleen, who
corrected more typographical errors than
I care to remember.*

To Our Readers:

We have been delighted with your enthusiastic response to Candlelight Ecstasy Romances®, and we thank you for the interest you have shown in this exciting series.

In the upcoming months we will continue to present the distinctive, sensuous love stories you have come to expect only from Ecstasy. We look forward to bringing you many more books from your favorite authors and also the very finest work from new authors of contemporary romantic fiction.

As always, we are striving to present the unique, absorbing love stories that you enjoy most—books that are more than ordinary romance.

Your suggestions and comments are always welcome. Please write to us at the address below.

Sincerely,

The Editors
Candlelight Romances
1 Dag Hammarskjold Plaza
New York, New York 10017

CHAPTER ONE

Brianna Douglas was frightened. She was very frightened. Sheer will power kept her clinging to a thin thread of control that prevented her from sinking into pure terror and a burning anger that anyone should dare to do this to her or any other human being. An anger that inspired her with the will to survive.

One of her captors aimed a careless kick in her direction and she cowered convincingly. Had he been less filled with a sense of power and a trifle more alert, it might have seemed odd to him that not a single whimper of pain passed her lips even though his heavy boot had connected with bruising force against her thigh. Bree gritted her teeth in a feral smile and allowed her head to fall forward against her chest. Let them think she was on the verge of collapse, it might make them careless.

She was, she realized, achingly tired. Every muscle in her body was protesting the abuse that had been heaped on it in the last eighteen hours. She longed to lay down and sink into a deep sleep. Conversely, she had to fight the urge to leap to her feet and run, anything to release the terrible tension that gripped her. She knew only too well that she wouldn't get very far.

To think that twenty-four hours ago she had been contemplating nothing more exciting than a good night's sleep. After doing some light housework in her one-bedroom apartment she had taken a long hot bath, a luxury that had been denied to her on her last assignment, and gone to bed early. She was looking forward to the next week of relaxation. After tramping through the South American jungles in search of animals that were more than elusive, they were downright invisible, she felt that she had earned some vacation time.

She had a luncheon date with her father tomorrow—no, that had been today that she had been due to have lunch with James Douglas, Colorado state senator. She wondered with a trace of amusement what his reaction had been when he was presented, not with his well-groomed daughter, but with an unkempt, bearded messenger informing him that his youngest child had been kidnapped.

He couldn't have had any more of a shock than she had had when she was rudely awakened from a sound sleep by a muffled crash in her living room. She had reacted with a calm born of spending much of her youth in some of the world's most politically unstable areas. She rolled over in bed and slid open the drawer of her nightstand, but she barely had time to get her hand on the small but deadly pistol that lay there when the door to her bedroom was thrown open and three stocky men burst into the room.

Moonlight flooded through the open curtains, lighting the scene with a milky brilliance. Bree was not a coward but she was also nobody's fool and, with the barrel of a rifle pointed at her, she obeyed the order, given in guttural English, to pull her hand out of the drawer very slowly. One of the intruders moved over and clicked on the bedside lamp before searching in the drawer to see what she had been after. Coming up with the gun, he snarled his contempt and swung his hand in a slap that knocked her against the headboard and left the taste of blood in her mouth.

A sharp command from the one who was apparently the leader stopped a second blow and the man stepped back reluctantly. Bree wiped the trickle of blood from her lip and tamped down the mixture of fright and rage that simmered inside her. Her demand for an explanation was ignored as if she hadn't spoken. Gesturing with the rifle, the leader told her to get up and get dressed for a trip to the mountains. Reluctantly, she swung her legs out of bed, furious at the lack of privacy and thankful that late September in Denver was cold enough to warrant the light pajamas she was wearing instead of her preferred sleeping attire, which was nothing. She dressed swiftly, pulling on a pair of heavy jeans and a long-sleeve flannel shirt over the pajamas.

She tried to think of some way to leave a message for those who would be looking for her but she was watched too carefully and the best she could hope for was that her brother Mark might notice that she had chosen to wear the soft knee-high Apache boots that were her favorite footwear for camping. It wasn't much to hope for but it was the best she had. Of course, even supposing he did realize where she had been taken, the Rocky Mountains was a rather large area to search with no other clues. She had better not depend on anybody but herself to get out of this.

She tied her hair up in a scarf to keep it out of the way, bundling the shoulder-length auburn curls up under the cotton square with no thought of style. She had barely finished the task when her arms were jerked behind her and she stifled a gasp of pain as her wrists were bound cruelly tight with a length of coarse rope that chafed at the delicate skin. Her captors all wore ski masks but they took the extra precaution of blindfolding her before they led her out of her apartment and down the stairs to shove her onto the floor of a waiting vehicle. She sent up a silent prayer that someone would see what was happening and call the police but she knew it was a forlorn hope. One of the reasons she had chosen this location was because it was quiet. There was rarely anyone about at four thirty in the afternoon, let alone at four thirty in the morning.

She could tell that she was in some kind of van from the amount of room inside, but they still did not take off the rag they had tied across her eyes. She supposed she ought to be grateful that they hadn't decided to gag her too.

Deprived of her sight, she found that her hearing and sense of smell seemed to become more acute. The latter she could have done without since it was immediately apparent that none of the men in the enclosed vehicle with her had more than a passing acquaintance with water and not even that much with soap.

She sat docilely on the floor and listened to the conversation going on among the kidnappers without drawing attention to herself. It was apparent that they didn't know she understood their language from the open way they spoke. Though it had been two years since her father had been a United States ambassador in their small Middle Eastern nation, Bree had no trouble following their conversation but she was careful to keep her expression blank. No sense in advertising her knowledge. She almost wished that she couldn't understand them. It was disconcerting, to say the least, to listen to them make plans for her eventual demise. But especially distressing was hearing what they planned before they killed her.

It was obvious that she would have to get away. They had no intention of returning her to her father alive and she would rather be shot trying to escape than become a plaything for them. They were going to kill her anyway, so she had nothing to lose.

Occasionally one of them would remember her presence and she endured with stoic acceptance the various kicks, slaps, and squeezes that came her way. She sensed their disappointment that she didn't scream or beg for mercy and she was glad to have denied them that much. She would play the game of accepting her fate but it was more than she could bring herself to do to whimper and whine for their entertainment, even if it would help to put them off their guard.

They had been driving around for several hours when the sound of the van's wheels changed. She was fairly sure that they had spent a lot of time just driving around Denver, but for the last hour or two they had been steadily climbing. The popping in her ears had told her that much but until now that had been her only clue as to where they were taking her. Now they were on a gravel road. Not that that told her much more. There were hundreds of gravel roads in the mountains and she had no way of knowing even the direction they had taken.

After what she estimated to be about a half hour, they came to a halt and she could hear them opening the back doors, letting in a rush of clean air that was more than welcome. She was jerked roughly to her feet and shoved out the door. Blindfolded and with her hands bound behind her back, she was unable to retain her balance and she fell facedown in the dirt to the evident amusement of her captors. One of them pulled her to her feet and she spit dirt out of her mouth, adding another mark to the growing tally in her mind. She strained her ears to catch some hint of their location but she could tell nothing specific. There was a good-size river somewhere close by. She could hear it rushing over its bed, but other than the smell of pine trees, that was the only clue she could detect.

They led her, stumbling and slipping, up a gravel slope and the sound of the river grew fainter behind them until it finally disappeared altogether as they entered the forest. Pine needles crunched under her feet and she breathed deeply of the fresh air, grateful to smell something besides the unwashed bodies of her captors. She had no way of knowing what time it was, but her stomach told her that it must be nearing lunchtime. They had been driving since five o'clock in the morning and she was both thirsty and hungry. She felt as if she had been stumbling around in the dark forever when they finally called a halt and she was allowed to sit down.

Someone yanked the blindfold off and she blinked and squinted against the light. When her eyes had adjusted she was able to see that it was not bright sunlight that had initially blinded her, but only a filtered version of it that came through the evergreen branches above her. She looked around the campsite and was forced to admit that they had chosen well—a small clearing in the pine forest which would be invisible from the air. In front of them a steep slope, bare of vegetation, stretched down to the river below. The road they had come in on was barely visible, just a narrow dirt track. The van was gone and she was left with her original three captors. The driver had presumably gone back to Denver to get her father's answer to their ransom demands.

She hoped that it singed their ears. She wondered if they really thought that he could grant amnesty to their compatriots who were currently in prison in the state of Colorado and then give them the money they were asking for and safe passage out of the country.

14

James Douglas was undeniably a power to be reckoned with in Colorado, but he certainly did not have the authority to give the terrorists what they planned to demand from him, and Bree knew her father well enough to know that even if it were within his power to give them what they asked, he wouldn't do it. It wasn't that he didn't love her—he did—but he had a strong sense of responsibility and, not even to save her life would he do something that was so patently wrong. He would also be well aware that the chances of ever seeing her alive were slim, even if he did comply with the kidnapper's demands. *She* knew from the conversations she had overheard that they had no intention of returning her alive.

The unprofessional way the whole thing had been carried out might have been amusing if it hadn't been so frightening. They hadn't even bothered to find out that her father couldn't do what they were asking of him even if he wanted to. Professional kidnappers might possibly have had some kind of a code of ethics, but these were nothing more than a bunch of unwashed, not-too-smart terrorists, and as such they were dangerously unpredictable.

It didn't seem to occur to any of them that she might be hungry or if it did, they didn't care. No one offered her anything to eat and she would have died before asking them for anything. One of them came over and poured some sour-tasting wine down her throat, laughing uproariously when it spilled onto her shirt, dampening the fabric until it clung to her. Bree felt her heart stop beating as he put his hand on her breast, ostensibly to feel how wet her shirt was, but she could see the animal gleam in his eyes and she knew what he was thinking. With her hands bound as they were, there would have been little she could have done to stop his advances, but one of the others called him away, telling him that there would be plenty of time for what he had in mind later. With a last cruel squeeze he let her go and moved over to join his companions and Bree released a quivering breath. She had to get away!

They had removed their ski masks, another indication that they weren't planning on letting her go, but she could see little of their features beyond the fact that they all wore scraggly beards and long hair. They untied her hands at dusk so that she could eat the stale sandwich they handed her, not out of compassion, but because none of them wanted to be bothered with feeding her. She supposed she should feel grateful that they hadn't just let her go hungry again. It took her almost ten minutes to work the circulation back into her hands until she could take hold of the sandwich and she bit her lip to restrain the moans of pain that the returning flow of blood brought to her lips. She ate slowly and when she was done she tucked her hands down by her sides. If she did nothing to draw attention to herself, maybe they would all assume that one of the others had tied her up again.

She repressed a shudder of revulsion as they discussed whether they should remove a finger or an ear to send to her father as proof that they had his daughter. It was not that she couldn't get along without either item, she thought with a touch of gallows humor. It was just that she had become rather attached to those portions of her anatomy over the years and she was not particularly anxious to lose either of them.

Whenever one of them happened to notice her existence, she was forced to endure their crude remarks, delivered in English so that she would be sure to understand what they were saying. The remarks she could ignore and

16

the various cuffs and kicks she could endure, but it was only with an effort of will that she was able to stay docile beneath the rough fondling that came her way. Her brother would have been proud of her, she thought savagely. Mark was always telling her that she ought to learn to control her temper.

Isolated as they were, the terrorists did not think it necessary to post a guard, and Bree feigned sleep until the three men had settled down in their sleeping bags. They apparently hadn't felt it necessary to provide her with any covering, though one of them did offer a lewd suggestion as to how she might keep warm.

The mountain air was cold but she barely noticed the chill as she slowly sat up. She inched her hand down her calf and slid open the narrow zipper that ran up the inside of one boot. It had nothing to do with securing the suede to her legs, the laces up the front did that. The zipper concealed a hidden pocket and she felt a surge of savage exultation when her fingers closed around the hilt of the small razor-sharp hunting knife that had lain concealed against her calf. The carved wooden handle felt warm against her palm and she itched to test its sharpness on the throats of the men who had brought her there, but she resisted the urge. She could never kill all three of them before they overpowered her and she was determined that they would not take her captive again. She would turn the knife against herself before she would let them take her.

She got to her feet silently and slid backward out of the clearing, careful not to look too intently at any one sleeping figure, letting her eyes shift across all of them. When she was out of sight she turned and began to make her way as swiftly as she could while trying to remain quiet. She had been slipping through the trees for only a few minutes when she heard an enraged shout go up behind her and knew that one of them must have awakened and discovered her escape. Her every instinct screamed, Run! But she kept to a steady, loping pace, the soft suede boots allowing her to move, if not in silence, then certainly more quietly than her pursuers in their heavy boots would be able to.

For over an hour she played cat and mouse with them. She kept her knife gripped in one hand, more for psychological reassurance than because it was doing her any good. As far as she could tell, there was only one of them still on her trail and he must be at least part bloodhound to have followed her this far. She wouldn't have known he was behind her except that she could hear an occasional crash when he stepped on a branch or slipped on the thick carpet of pine needles.

She turned to look over her shoulder, moving backward as she tried to see some flicker of movement or light if he was using a flashlight. She had taken no more than three steps when her heel connected with something unyielding. She tucked herself into a ball as she began to fall, rolling backward over the obstruction and doing a complete somersault before coming to her feet in a half-crouch, her knife in hand. She knew she had tripped over a man before she landed on her feet and her only thought was that somehow one of them had managed to circle around in front of her and had been waiting for her.

The figure that had come to a sitting position in the sleeping bag was definitely not one of her former captors, that much was obvious just by his outline.

"If you're planning on using that thing, honey, you'd better be good with it because I'm not going to make it easy." The voice was rough, gravelly, and unmistakably

American. Bree relaxed slightly and sought to make out something more than a vague outline. So intent was she on trying to see something more of the stranger that she didn't notice the hand that lay on top of the sleeping bag, a large pistol in its grip.

"I'm sorry. I didn't mean to startle you. I thought you were someone else."

"That's comforting. I'd hate to think that a strange young woman should have some reason to try to kill me." There was a definite vein of amusement in the attractive voice that might have intrigued her at another time, but she was barely listening now. She stood up fully and turned in the direction she had just come. She was no Daniel Boone, but that last crack of sound had been closer than she liked. She couldn't linger any longer. She had turned to leave when it occurred to her that the stranger might be in danger if her pursuer should stumble over him as she had. She owed him a warning. She turned to him briskly and then took an involuntary step back. He had crawled out of the sleeping bag and now stood next to her, looking back toward where she had come from. Even in the pale moonlight his size was imposing. It was not so much his height, though he was at least two inches over the six-foot mark, but he was immensely broad, his shoulders seeming to go on forever.

She shook her head. What difference did it make if he were as big as King Kong? He was still an innocent tourist who had been caught up in her affairs through no fault of his own and she couldn't just leave him without a warning.

She spoke rapidly. "Listen, I know this is going to sound melodramatic, but this is a very unhealthy place to camp. I would strongly suggest that you pack up your things and get out of here as quickly as possible. Is your car nearby?" She had a fleeting hope that if he had a car close then maybe all her problems would be solved, but he shook his head and the hope faded.

"I hiked in. My car is about a two-day walk away from here." He sounded apologetic but there was still an underlying tone of amusement.

She shrugged. "I suppose it was too much to hope for. If you're smart, you'll hightail it back there and get out of here. When you get back to civilization, contact the Denver police department and tell them where you saw me. I'm sure there'll be a reward or something."

She turned away but was stopped by the massive hand that came down on her shoulder. She turned back, her mouth open to deliver a scathing tirade.

"I'd be happy to tell them where I saw you, but don't you think I ought to know who you are and what you're running from?"

She gave a half laugh at her own stupidity. "I'm Bree Douglas and the less you know about what I'm running from, the better for you. Suffice it to say that there are some rather nasty characters looking for me and if they find you . . . well, they seem the type to shoot first and ask questions later. I would appreciate it if you would just take my word that you are in real danger and get out of the way before you get caught up in something you can't handle. The last thing I need right now is to have a helpless tourist on my hands."

She thought she heard a faint laugh from her unwelcome companion, but a muffled curse nearby caught her attention and she gestured sharply to him to be silent. She moved slowly to the edge of his camp nearest where the sound had come from. There he was. She caught the gleam of moonlight off his rifle barrel. If she had been alone, she might have tried to outrun her pursuer, but she couldn't leave an innocent bystander alone to face an insane terrorist. Besides, perhaps it would be best to delay this one if she could. That would give her time to get farther away before the others had a chance to catch up with her.

She took a few deep calming breaths and murmured a small prayer of thanks that the stranger did not have a fire going. At least she wasn't backlit by the flames. Stay calm, she told herself, trying to imagine that she was safe at home in a martial arts class. This was nothing more than a routine exercise, she thought. Just a simple exercise. Never mind that her life and that of the stranger might depend on it; this was still just a simple exercise. She could see him clearly now. He was not taking any precautions against being seen. Of course, he would never expect the mouse to turn and bite the cat. He was moving directly toward her and she relaxed her muscles and waited until he was in the right position before she moved. Balancing on her right leg, she kicked her left leg straight out and swung it around. It caught him squarely across the midriff with the force of an iron bar and he bent over in a woof of agony. Bree brought her clenched fists, with the haft of her knife gripped between them, down across his vulnerable nape, and he collapsed onto the ground at her feet.

Her breath came in deep gasps, less from exertion than from the sudden release of tension and the feeling of exultation that swept through her. She had won! She had defeated the enemy, even if it was only one of them. She turned away from her victim but stopped at a quiet suggestion from the stranger. "You ought to take his gun."

Grimacing at not having thought of it herself, she leaned over and pulled the rifle out from underneath the limp body, suppressing the urge to gag at the stench of his unwashed clothing.

When she turned back to her companion she saw that he had rapidly and efficiently rolled up his sleeping bag and thrust it and a few other things into his pack. He was lacing on his boots. "My car is down the canyon. With luck we should be able to get there in a day and a half."

She drew herself up to her full five feet six inches and then had to tilt her head back to look at him as he got to his feet. "Look, I appreciate the offer but it's not you they're interested in, it's me. If you just get out of my way, then they'll leave you alone and follow me, if any of them is capable of it."

He didn't appear to be listening as he turned to make a last sweeping survey of his camp. His eyes paused on the body. "Did you kill him?" He asked the question without any concern, only mild interest. His bland acceptance of the fact that she might have just killed a man seemed perfectly normal to Bree in her current state.

"I don't think so but, to tell the truth, I don't really care. I really do wish you'd just go on your way and forget about me." He didn't answer but she could read determination in the set of his broad shoulders and, with a faint sigh, she gave in. She was too tired to argue with him. "I suppose it might be best if we went together. They might mistake the trail and end up following you and I'd hate for them to come on you when I wasn't there. But really, the last thing I needed at this point in my life was to pick up a tourist and get someone else involved. It's just the final disaster in a day that was not one of my best to begin with.

I've got enough trouble just trying to look out for my own neck."

Again there was that quiet laugh, but his voice was sober, almost meek. "Don't worry about me. I won't get in your way."

He turned to lead the way out of the clearing, ignoring her muttered, "I just bet you won't."

CHAPTER TWO

The next four or five hours were to remain forever a blur in Bree's memory. The feeling of exhilaration that had filled her with energy after her defeat of one of her former captors had drained away, leaving her tired and achingly aware of every bruise. She followed the stranger without protest, assuming that he knew where he was going. It occurred to her sometime after they started that she didn't even know his name and that, for an ordinary camper, he hadn't seemed to be overly disconcerted by her precipitate entrance into his life. She grappled with this point briefly and then decided that perhaps he was an off-duty police officer or someone similarly trained to cope with the unexpected. She considered asking him to settle the issue but then decided that it was not worth the effort.

The pace he had set was not brutal and, under ordinary circumstances, Bree could have kept it up for hours without tiring, but she was emotionally and physically exhausted and it was pure will power that kept her on her feet and moving. That and the knowledge that while she had dealt with one of the terrorists with relative ease, there was certainly no guarantee that her luck would hold in a second encounter. Common sense dictated that they put as much distance as possible between themselves and their pursuers.

The weight of the rifle she had taken from the body of the terrorist seemed to drag her down and once or twice

24

she came out of a half stupor to find that she had slid the strap off her shoulder and was on the verge of dropping the weapon by the wayside. She gritted her teeth and concentrated on naming all the presidents in order to stay awake. From there she went on to naming all the states and their capitals and she was in the middle of trying to remember the capital of Maine when she almost ran into her companion, her concentration such that she hadn't even realized that he had stopped.

She shook herself awake and looked around, surprised to see that while she had been devoting her energies to staying on her feet the sun had risen over the horizon and it was now quite light out.

"We'll stop here for now. We can camp for the day and then start out again at dusk. With any luck we should be able to reach my car by dawn tomorrow." He shrugged off his pack as he spoke and Bree blinked tiredly while she watched him unload it.

"I don't know your name."

His back was turned to her as he unrolled his sleeping bag and she examined what she could see of him without interest. If the front of him was any kind of a match for his back, then he should be a remarkably attractive man, she thought. His hair was very thick and just faintly wavy and, where the early morning sunlight caught it, it raised almost blue highlights in its inky blackness. There was a scattering of gray there, too, so he wasn't a young man, but she had already guessed that from his voice. There had been an element of command in it that could only come with years of experience. When he got to his feet and turned to face her, she was distantly pleased to see that her estimation had been right. He was a very attractive man. Tall, dark, and handsome was the description that came immediately to mind but she dismissed it as being too anemic. Tall and dark—yes. But handsome was not the right word. Sexy, she decided. That suited him more than handsome. His face was craggy and deep-set eyes and thick eyebrows combined to conceal the expression in a pair of dark brown eyes that, at another time, might have made her vividly aware of her femininity. His nose was a bold slant with a distinct bump in the middle of it where it had been broken and improperly set, she imagined, and his well-shaped mouth had a twist to it that bespoke a deeply sensuous nature.

Her first impression of his size was carried out in daylight. At least two inches over six feet and with shoulders that could easily have graced a linebacker for the Denver Broncos. Her gaze traveled down his body, across his flat stomach and strong thighs to his feet, encased in a pair of sturdy hiking boots. Her exhausted mind registered something and returned to his jean-clad hips. A very serviceable pistol sat snugly in a well-worn holster and from the comfortable way it rested there, it was obvious that he was quite accustomed to carrying it.

"Sean Mallory." She refocused her eyes on his face as she tried to decipher the meaning of his apparently meaningless statement. "You wanted to know what my name was," he reminded her gently. "Sean Mallory."

Bree felt her knees begin to buckle and she fought to retain consciousness as she sagged to the ground. Her knees had barely hit the soft pine carpet when he was beside her, lifting her in his arms as if she weighed no more than an infant and carrying her to where he had spread the sleeping bag.

"I don't think you'll get in the way after all," she murmured dreamily as her eyes began to close. She felt rather than heard the rich chuckle that resonated in his chest.

"I never said I would."

He laid her down carefully and she almost cried aloud at the relief of not having to take another step. The down sleeping bag felt like heaven to her and she snuggled into it, vaguely aware of someone unlacing her boots and unbuckling her belt. "I don't suppose you know what the capital of Maine is?" But she was asleep before he could answer her.

Sean zipped the sleeping bag up around her and set her boots to one side, admiring the workmanship that had allowed her to conceal a knife right in the midst of the kidnappers. She was quite a woman. He glanced at her sleeping face. She certainly had guts. He grinned, remembering her irritation at the thought of having to protect him. It had been a long time since anyone had thought it necessary to worry about protecting him.

He glanced around the campsite he had chosen, automatically taking note of the vulnerable areas where an enemy could attack. He should have asked her how many of them they might have to contend with. It would also have been nice to know who "they" were. He sat down with his back against a boulder and chewed on a piece of jerky from his pack. They had plenty of food to get them through until tomorrow morning and, if necessary, they could manage for a couple of weeks. He had planned to spend quite a while in the mountains and he had brought plenty of provisions with him. Hopefully they wouldn't need to worry about it, but he was well aware that it was never smart to count on things going the way you wanted them to. Better to prepare for the worst and then be pleasantly surprised.

His mind sifted methodically through what little information he had. She had said her name was Bree Douglas and that the Denver police would be interested in knowing where she was. She had also said that there would probably be a reward offered for any information. Those facts indicated that she had been kidnaped and that her family was wealthy enough that they could afford to offer a reward. The obvious conclusion was that she had been kidnapped for ransom but he suspected that it wasn't that simple.

The rifle she had taken from the man she had knocked out was a military weapon and the man had been wearing a uniform jacket. Probably some kind of pseudomilitary terrorist group, he decided, but why would they kidnap a young American woman? What would they have to gain? Money? Possibly. But such organizations were generally after more than money. So what could Bree Douglas or her family offer that they might want? His eyebrows drew together as he considered the fact that *James* Douglas was a state senator. A coincidence? Maybe, but he didn't think so.

He turned slightly to look down the slope, thus bringing the sleeping woman into his line of vision. He scanned the slide scar below them and then let his eyes return to the much pleasanter view near at hand. Exhaustion had etched dark circles beneath her eyes and had driven the color from her cheeks, but she was still an exceptionally attractive young woman, he admitted. The scarf over her hair had become dislodged and one auburn curl had escaped its confines to fall across her broad forehead, making her skin look creamy white in contrast to its fiery warmth. Her finely arched brows were a rich sable color, as were the long curly eyelashes that lay in soft crescents on her cheeks. Her eyes were a dark sapphire blue, he remembered from his brief glimpse of them before she collapsed. Her nose was short and straight and her mouth was a richly modeled curve that seemed to be made for kissing. Her body now concealed by the sleeping bag had been light but well-rounded and he decided that she would probably look good in a bikini or, better yet, stretched out on a pair of satin sheets.

Hold it! He braked his errant thoughts and his dark brows almost met over his nose in a frown. Let's not have any of that. The woman had enough problems without having to deal with amorous advances from someone she had done her best to protect. Besides, she was much too young for him.

It was late afternoon before Bree began to stir. She came awake slowly, her nose twitching as the smell of beef broth wafted across her face. Her stomach rumbled a protest and she blinked open her eyes, momentarily disconcerted by the canopy of pine boughs over her head. A noise off to the side drew her attention and she focused on a man's broad back bent over a tiny fire set beneath the lee of a rock outcropping. Recent events washed over her consciousness and she stifled a groan. What a pity that it hadn't all been some kind of a weird dream.

She sat up and pulled the scarf off her head, running her fingers through the tousled curls and grimacing at their tangled condition. She was trying to finger-comb some of the knots out when a massive hand came into her line of vision, holding a small pocket comb.

She glanced up, startled that a man of his size could move so quietly. He smiled down at her and dropped the comb onto the sleeping bag in front of her. "Sorry I can't offer you a brush, but this should help some." He nodded pleasantly in answer to her murmured thanks and moved back to the fire. "Soup should be ready soon if you're hungry."

He didn't seem to expect an answer to his comment and she didn't offer one, letting her eyes follow him around the tiny clearing while she worked the tangles out of her hair with his comb. His quiet efficiency as he went about preparing a meal over the fire and his calm alertness as he kept an eye on the surrounding area made it obvious that this was not an entirely new game to him.

Her hair once more falling in richly hued curls to her shoulders, Bree climbed out of the sleeping bag, flushing slightly as she resnapped her jeans and buckled the belt he had undone so that she could sleep more comfortably. She appreciated his consideration but it seemed distressingly intimate to think that he had literally put her to bed. She didn't even know the man's name! Or did she? Hadn't he told her his name this morning before she conked out? Now, what had it been? Sean! That was it. Sean Mallory. She sat back down to pull on her boots, checking to make sure that her knife was in its proper place before tying the laces.

"That's a clever trick." She glanced up to see him gesturing to her footwear. "Do you often get into situations where you need a concealed weapon?"

She grinned as she got to her feet, trying to ignore the aches and pains that a few hours sleep had allowed to set into her bones. "Believe it or not, this is a first. My brother had them made for me because I kept borrowing his hunting knife and losing it. He thought maybe if it was attached, it wouldn't come loose so often. I must say, I was grateful to him yesterday morning.

"Did you say something about soup?" She moved over

to the fire and eyed the small pot hopefully. Her stomach was asking loudly if her throat had been cut; the memory of the stale sandwich she had had the night before had faded into the distance. There was only one mug and Sean insisted that she eat first since he had had a chance to have something while she slept. Bree protested, but it was a half-hearted effort at best, and she sipped at the beef broth with delicate greed, using the spoon he gave her to scoop up the vegetables when the broth was gone.

He waited until she had appeased her appetite somewhat before speaking. "We didn't get a chance to do much talking last night. Perhaps I'm doing him an injustice, considering our very brief acquaintance, but I assume the guy you very neatly knocked out this morning was not a friend of yours?"

Bree gave him a rueful smile. "That's putting it mildly. He helped to kidnap me."

"Why?"

She took another swallow of broth before answering. "Well, you see, my father is James Douglas, the senator." She glanced at him and he nodded to indicate that he recognized the name. "They had some crazy idea that being a senator gave him the power to grant amnesty to some of their friends." She shrugged. "Of course, it doesn't, but they didn't bother to find that out before deciding that it would be a good idea to kidnap me. I think they just picked on Dad because he was an ambassador to their country for a few years before it got so unstable that our government closed the embassy. They knew his name and knew he was in the government now and that's as far as they looked."

"What country?"

She named a small Middle-Eastern nation well known for its political instability, and he nodded.

"They broke into my apartment last night—no, I guess it was the night before last. Time is a little mixed up right now. Anyway, they broke in and hauled me off at gunpoint. They didn't know that I understood their language, so they talked pretty openly about their plans.

"I was supposed to have lunch with my father today, I mean yesterday, and one of them was going to show up in my place to present their demands. I hope Dad had him hauled off and fed to a German shepherd."

Sean chuckled and she looked at him with a slightly self-conscious grin. "I suppose that sounds a little bloodthirsty, but it's the way I feel right now. I guess I'm not very good at turning the other cheek."

She continued after a moment. "After Dad had given them what they wanted, they were going to have their fun with me and then dump my body in a nice remote spot." She managed to speak casually but her companion noted the shudder of revulsion that shook her briefly. His estimation of her went up several degrees. She really was one hell of a woman.

When her appetite had been satisfied, she handed the mug to him, and while he ate she put a question or two of her own. She gestured gracefully to the revolver at his side. "It seems apparent that you aren't quite the helpless tourist I took you for last night and something tells me that you could have broken my determined friend in two without exerting yourself." He shrugged but didn't deny it. "May I ask who you are and just what you were doing camped in the middle of my escape route?"

He set down the empty mug and leaned back against a boulder, his eyes moving restlessly over the area outside their camp before coming back to her. "I told you my name this morning before you passed out. Actually your guess that I was a tourist wasn't really off. I am a tourist. I came up here to spend a quiet two or three weeks camping. As for the gun"—he paused and then shrugged again —"I wear a gun in my line of work. I'd feel rather naked without it. Besides, it's not wise to camp by yourself without some means of protection." His tone made it clear that as far as he was concerned the subject was closed. Bree gave a mental shrug. If he didn't want to talk about his work, then it was certainly no business of hers.

She changed the subject. "I suppose I should have asked this when I woke up, but I didn't think of it. Where am I?"

He blinked, startled, and then smiled at her. "I didn't stop to think that they probably didn't give you a roadmap. You're several miles up the Cache la Poudre River canyon."

"Cache la Poudre. Let's see." She thought for a moment. "My high school French tells me that's hide the powder and my shaky geography tells me that we're north of Denver. Am I right?"

"On the nose. By the way, you didn't tell me how you managed to escape."

"Nothing too spectacular really. When they decided to let me eat, none of them wanted to have to feed me bite by bite, so they untied my hands and gave me a sandwich." She rubbed her wrists, remembering the tingling pain of returning circulation. "I had been pretty quiet and I hadn't given them any trouble. I guess they thought I was pretty well subdued. When I was done eating, I held my hands together like they were tied and apparently they all assumed that someone else had tied me up again. I

33

waited until they were all asleep and then I slipped out of their camp and took off running. It was lucky for me that none of them was any faster than they were."

She shrugged lightly, as if to dismiss the subject, and changed the topic. "You seem to be pretty familiar with this area. Do you live around here?"

"I have a ranch in eastern Colorado. I don't spend much time there though. I have a good man to run it. I just like to know as much as possible about an area I'm spending time in. I guess I've picked up quite a bit of information over the years."

He didn't offer any more information than that and after a moment Bree asked another question. "How far is it to your car?"

"With luck we should still be able to get there by about dawn tomorrow."

She picked up the uneasiness in his rough voice and turned a questioning look on him. "What's wrong? You sound like you don't expect luck to be with us."

"I'm not expecting anything. I've learned the hard way that it's best to plan for the worst and then you can be pleasantly surprised if it doesn't happen."

He set about dousing their tiny campfire and Bree realized that the day was almost gone. Purple shadows were creeping out of the pine forest around them and a chill evening breeze had sprung up. She shivered, her flannel shirt suddenly seeming woefully thin. Last night she had been too tired to notice the cold, but she had a feeling that tonight she was not going to be so lucky.

"Here." She glanced up, startled again by his silent approach. He was holding out a thick shirt. "I pack light, so I didn't bring anything heavier than this, but it should help some." Bree shrugged into the dark blue garment gratefully, stifling a laugh at the picture she must have presented, with the tails hanging almost to her knees and the cuffs ending somewhere below her hands. She looked up and caught a glimpse of even white teeth as Sean shared her amusement. "You look like an orphan. Let me roll up those sleeves so you can find your hands."

She sat still, obediently holding out her arm as he knelt next to her so that he could fold the cuffs back until her hands emerged. In the fading light he had to move close to see what he was doing, his dark head bent over the task. Bree let her eyes roam freely over his face, admiring the strong lines of experience that bracketed his mouth. The dark hair at his temples was tinged with silver and she had a sudden urge to run her fingers through it. He finished the second sleeve and straightened, the light remark dying on his lips as his eyes met hers. One large hand came out to touch a darkening bruise along her jaw, his finger tracing the delicate curve before his hand cupped her chin. Bree shivered, not with cold, but with the sudden surge of desire that coursed through her veins. Kidnaping and terrorists all faded into the distance; her entire being concentrated on the man in front of her.

His thumb rubbed across her mouth and her lips parted, inviting his kiss. He leaned toward her and her eyes fluttered shut, her hands moving up to clasp his shoulders as she waited, trembling with anticipation, to feel his mouth touch hers. His lips touched hers briefly before moving to press softly against the bruise that marred her smooth skin. She felt him moving away and opened her eyes to see him kneeling back in front of her, his expression unreadable in the near dark but his voice husky with restraint. "Isn't that supposed to cure a bruise? Kiss and make it well?"

She stifled her aching disappointment and managed a lopsided grin. "You don't look at all like my mother."

"Well, thank God for small favors," he murmured fervently and the tense moment was gone. He got to his feet before extending a hand to help her up. She couldn't quite stifle a moan of pain as her bruised thigh protested her movement and Sean's hand was immediately under her elbow, supporting her. "Are you hurt?"

She shook her head and straightened away from his support, biting her lip against the sharp stab of pain that quickly subsided into a dull ache. "Just a bruise. I'll be okay once we get started. It'll loosen up with a little movement." He hesitated, as if considering, and then said nothing more. She knew as well as he did that they couldn't just stay where they were without risking discovery. As long as she could move they had to cover ground.

Sean shrugged his pack over his broad shoulders and then bent to pick up the confiscated rifle. He turned to hand it to her and then paused. "Do you know how to use this?"

There was no patronization in his voice, just an honest question and Bree accepted it as such. "Mark taught me to shoot when I was eighteen. This one's a little heavier than what I'm used to, but I can handle it."

Without further question he handed her the weapon and then checked to make sure that he could reach his pistol without any interference from his pack. He turned to sweep the camp one last time before letting his eyes settle on her. "Ready?" She nodded and he set out immediately, angling his path so that they would stay at the edge of the slide scar, just within the trees.

CHAPTER THREE

Bree followed close on Sean's heels until the moon came up and she could make out something of the path they were following. He must have eyes like a cat to be able to see where he was going in this pitch blackness, she thought.

She had been right about her aches and pains; they did ease up with movement. They didn't disappear entirely, but they faded to a bearable ache. By tomorrow, she knew, she'd be every color of the rainbow. One of the curses of being so fair-skinned was the fact that she bruised easily. Mark had once complained that all you had to do was look at her and she turned purple. She smiled at the memory of his youthful complaint, delivered after a game of touch football in which she had refused to let him have the ball. Being a practical young man, even at eighteen, he had simply picked her up, thrown her over his shoulder, and carried her across the goal line. The resulting bruises hadn't bothered Bree at all. She had been more upset by the fact that he had, in her opinion, cheated, but he did receive a thorough scolding from their mother.

She stumbled over a dead branch and caught her breath on a gasp of pain as she threw all her weight onto her bruised thigh. Sean looked over his shoulder and she nodded that she was all right. She thought longingly of a nice hot bath. She was filthy and she longed to scrub away the dirt and soak away her aches. If they could get to his car by morning, she should be able to have that bath tomorrow.

She let her thoughts drift to the man ahead of her. There was an arrogance in his stride that indicated he was in complete control of himself and everything around him. What did he do for a living that required him to carry a gun? She was positive he wasn't a policeman. If he were, he wouldn't be so cagy about admitting it. So what did that leave? F.B.I.? C.I.A? Some other government agency? Bodyguard? Somehow none of those quite fit the picture she had of him. He was too independent to be a mere agent for anybody. Head of some sort of spy division? Did spies even come in divisions?

Her thoughts leapfrogged to a new subject. Why hadn't he kissed her? He had wanted to, she was positive of that. That web of sensual awareness had not been her imagination, and she had been more than willing, yet he had drawn back. And that was another thing. Why had she been so willing? She had never been the kind to give or receive easy kisses, a strong sense of self-respect making her very particular about whom she kissed. But all Sean had done was touch her cheek and she would have fallen into bed with him in an instant—if there had been a bed nearby. She had never before met a man who could generate so much sexual electricity with a mere touch. It was probably just as well that she wouldn't be spending much more time alone with him. She might be tempted to fall into a casual affair for the first time in her life.

They made good time, keeping up a steady pace with only two brief rest stops during the night. Still, the sun was well up in the sky before Sean called a halt. Bree moved up beside him and looked to where he pointed. Never had a vehicle of any kind looked so beautiful! She would have thought it lovely had it been a beat-up jalopy. Anything that would get her home safely. But, as a matter of fact, it was a beautiful car under any circumstances. A deep midnight-blue Mercedes 450SL sat in solitary elegance in the gravel lay-by where he had parked it.

Bree felt her muscles begin to sag with relief. At last the end of the nightmare was in sight! But when she would have started down the slope, Sean put out a hand to stop her. She glanced up, impatient to get to the safety of the car, but he anticipated her question.

"If your friends got here ahead of us, they may have someone watching the car. They may or may not know that you and I are together, but they probably aren't going to take a chance on you just getting into a car and driving off." He waited until she gave a nod of agreement, sensing the logic of his statement. "I'll go down to the car, just like an ordinary camper about to drive home after a camping trip. You wait until you see me start the car and give you a thumbs-up sign, then you get down there as fast as you can. I'll have your door open. Stay as low as possible and run in a zigzag pattern."

Bree nodded, a shiver of fear going up her spine as she realized that he was afraid they might try to kill her. Sean's hand under her chin tipped her face up to his and he smiled down into her wide blue eyes. "Don't worry, honey. Chances are they haven't found the car, and even if they did, they may not make any connection. In a few minutes you'll be sitting in air-conditioned comfort and all of this will be just a bad dream."

He bent his head and kissed her gently, reassuringly. At least that was his intention. But Bree's mouth softened invitingly under his and, with a muffled groan, he put one arm around her shoulders to draw her against him. Her eyes closed and she inhaled his scent, a faint musky smell that aroused all of her senses. Her hands gripped his shoulders and she strained her body upward in an attempt to get still closer to him, her mouth parting eagerly beneath the aggressive thrust of his tongue. Her hands moved from his shoulders to bury themselves in his hair, her fingers sliding through its silky thickness.

Gently but inexorably Sean drew back, his hands moving to her shoulders to hold her at a distance. Bree opened weighted eyelids and looked at him blankly. "You could make a saint forget everything but that mouth of yours, but I don't think this is the time or the place for this sort of thing." The rueful amusement in his voice brought her back to a sense of where they were and she was stunned when she realized that she had completely forgotten their danger. Sean touched her cheek with one callused fingertip before turning and ducking under a low branch to start down the slope to his car.

With an effort Bree pulled her scattered wits together and crouched down into a position where she could watch him without being seen herself. He moved down the slope with apparent casualness, no looking over his shoulder, no suspicious glances into the underbrush, and it wasn't until she had watched him for a few minutes that she realized that he was presenting a very poor target for anyone hidden in the canyon around them. He moved from one patch of trees and shrubs to the shadow of a boulder and he was always moving in a random zigzag pattern. Yet, he was presenting the picture of a casual hiker with consummate skill.

That wasn't the only thing he was skilled in, she thought ruefully as she watched him reach his car and unlock the door without incident. She touched her mouth with the tip of one finger. She had not reached the age of twenty-eight without experiencing her share of passionate kisses, but she had never been kissed like that. Her toes had literally curled with pleasure and her body still tingled with heightened awareness.

She refocused her attention on Sean, her arched brows drawing together in a concerned frown as she watched him get out of the car and open the hood. He leaned over the fender to inspect the engine compartment and Bree found herself leaning forward with him, as if she could see inside the car.

Her entire attention was focused on the man below and she didn't hear the stealthy footsteps until they were right behind her. The snapping of a small twig beneath a heavy boot alerted her to the danger and she tried to come to her feet and turn around at the same time but the move was only half completed when she was knocked to the ground by a man's body. She struggled furiously to get her hands into a position to defend herself, but her arms were pinned to the ground beneath her own weight. Fetid breath wafted across her face, almost gagging her as she writhed impotently beneath her assailant's crushing weight.

Bree was strong but he held her pinned down easily, his legs clamping around her hips and her own weight trapping her arms. He laughed cruelly, raising one hand to deliver a casual slap across her face that made her ears ring. His fingers fumbled with the top buttons of her outer shirt and she renewed her struggles as she felt his rising excitement at having her helpless beneath him. He muttered something in his native language as the buttons on the heavy shirt gave way, only to disclose her own shirt beneath. Though several choice epithets came to mind, she didn't waste her breath in discussing his doubtful ancestry. Her strength was giving out and her breath came in deep gasping sobs as she fought to get loose.

His hand came up again and she closed her eyes as it began to descend toward her face, bracing herself for its impact. It never landed. The terrorist's crushing weight was suddenly lifted and her eyes flew open in time to see him hurtling a short distance through the air before coming to an abrupt halt against a tree trunk. He staggered drunkenly to his feet, groping for his holstered gun, but he didn't get a chance to draw it before Sean reached him again.

Bree buttoned her shirt with fingers that shook, fumbling for several seconds with one buttonhole before it dawned on her that the button was gone, ripped off by her attacker. Her eyes avoided the one-sided battle in progress a few feet away and she was still sitting on the ground staring at her shaking hands when Sean touched her on the shoulder.

"Are you all right?" She nodded in answer to the rasping question, obeying the tug of his hand and getting to her feet. Her eyes touched on the still figure a few feet away.

"Is he dead?" She was vaguely surprised at the sound of her own voice. Only a slight tremor betrayed its calm tone.

"Yes." Sean answered briefly, ignoring the body as he swooped to pick up the rifle she had set aside on seeing the car. His hard fingers closed around her slim wrist and Bree looked up at him questioningly. Leashed tension shimmered like a force field around him and his eyes blazed almost gold with it. "We've got to put some distance between us and the car. They found it and I don't know if they know that we're together but they aren't taking any chances. They took the rotor." She looked at him blankly

42

and he explained with controlled impatience. "Without the rotor the car won't start. Now, would you get a move on?"

He enforced his command with a firm tug on her captured wrist. Bree forced her thoughts away from the still body nearby and moved forward obediently. If they couldn't use his car, then he was right in saying that they needed to put some distance between themselves and the now useless Mercedes. She matched his loping stride easily for the next half hour. It was gradually sinking into her consciousness that the aura of tension that surrounded him was not just the natural energy of a victorious warrior. Surely that would have faded by now, but it still shimmered almost visibly around him when he came to a halt two or three miles away. She had opened her mouth to ask him if something was wrong, when he turned to her, his rugged features set in lines of forbidding anger.

"Now, would you mind telling me just what in the hell you were trying to prove back there?" He directed the question at her but Bree almost looked around to see if he could possibly be talking to someone else.

"Me?" She squeaked out the question. He must be talking to somebody else.

"Who else would I be talking to?" he asked with withering sarcasm.

Obviously he was unhinged, she decided. That was the only reasonable explanation. After all, she had only known him a short while and maniacs often seemed sane until something sent them over the edge. She answered cautiously, not wanting to say anything that might make him violent.

"I—I'm not sure I know what you mean. Why should I be trying to prove anything?" She edged away as she spoke, anxious to put a little distance between them but Sean reached out and snagged her wrist in an unbreakable hold, bringing her firmly in front of him and pinning her there with his angry gaze.

"That's what I'd like to know. Don't look at me like you don't know what I'm talking about." She did her best to look as if she knew what he was talking about but he wasn't convinced. He transferred his hold to her shoulders and the tensile strength of his fingers gave her the impression that it was only with an effort that he restrained his urge to shake her until her teeth rattled. "You do admit that that scummy little acquaintance of yours had you well and truly pinned? That you couldn't have gotten away from him without help?"

Bree almost sighed aloud in her relief. So that's what it was! He was upset because she hadn't thanked him. Well, there had hardly been an opportunity until now but there was no real need to point that out. If he wanted gratitude, he could have it, heartfelt and sincere.

"I want to tell you how grateful I am. I know *thank you* doesn't seem like mu—" An angry curse halted her in mid-word.

"I don't want your gratitude, you nitwit!"

She blinked in surprise. If he didn't want her gratitude, what did he want? Maybe her first guess had been right and he *was* nuts. The grip on her shoulders tightened as Sean sought to control his anger. He leaned down until they were at eye level and spoke clearly and concisely as if talking to an idiot.

"If you admit that you couldn't handle him alone, why didn't you scream for help?" She looked at him blankly and he all but ground his teeth with frustration. "You must have known that I would have heard you, but I

44

didn't hear a sound. I had no idea that you were in trouble until I saw you! Why didn't you scream?"

"I didn't think of it." Her honest answer did not appease him. In fact, it seemed to make him angrier, if anything.

"You didn't think of it? Just what did you think of?"

"All I thought of was trying to get away. It just never occurred to me to scream." Apparently his male ego was bruised. Well, he had earned a little soothing if that's what he needed. "I'm used to depending on nobody but myself, Sean. I guess in the struggle I just didn't remember that I had somebody else I could depend on." She tried her best apologetic female voice and even managed to hang her head a little.

"Don't give me that pathetic little-woman act. You're a stubborn, independent woman and someone should have shaken some sense into you when you were five years old. It's probably too late to do any good now." There was a trace of wistfulness in his rough voice that said he'd like to try it anyway.

Bree's head came up and she met his eyes with a hint of anger in hers. She had apologized. She was damned if she'd grovel. This arrogant male needn't think he was her superior just because he had muscles like a gorilla.

"You don't have to give me that defiant look. I've already admitted it's too late to shake any sense into you. But if you had the sense of a pea hen, you would have screamed."

"I suppose that if it had been you who was in trouble, you'd have screamed for help?"

Sean opened his mouth and then shut it. His expression changed from anger to astonishment to dawning amusement in rapid succession. A deep tuck appeared in one

45

lean cheek as he fought to keep his expression solemn, but his eyes fairly danced with laughter. There was only a slight quiver in his voice when he answered her. "Of course I would have. I'd have kicked and screamed and pulled his hair and probably tried to scratch him."

The sudden vision of a man of his size kicking and screaming was too much for Bree and she burst into laughter. He could not restrain his own amusement any longer and they laughed until Bree thought she would cry. Every time she stopped, her eyes would meet his and it would set her off again. They had long since collapsed onto the ground when they finally managed to stop laughing.

A huge yawn caught Bree by surprise, reminding her that her sleep yesterday was a long time ago. Sean got to his feet and stretched tiredly and she realized that he hadn't had any sleep since she had stumbled into his camp the night before last. He had to be exhausted, she thought guiltily, and yet it didn't show except in the faint hollowness around his eyes.

"We'd better get started. I want to put a couple more miles behind us before we break for lunch and, if you think you're up to it, I'd like to keep going until dark. I think the one who jumped you was left to keep an eye on the car just in case you showed up. The others are probably still out beating the bush for you. We can make better time if we travel during the day, so we'll chance it that they're a long way behind us and sleep tonight and travel tomorrow."

Bree got to her feet and stretched. She winced as she discovered several new bruises. She was going to be black and blue and probably green and yellow, too, by tomorrow.

"Did he hurt you?"

She looked up and saw real concern in his dark eyes. She shrugged and then wished she hadn't. Her shoulders had taken the brunt of the recent battle and they let her know, in no uncertain terms, that shrugs were a foolish indulgence. She managed what she hoped was a natural smile.

"Not really. Just a few more bruises. They'll never be noticed among the old crop. Sean, I really do want to thank you for what you did back there." He frowned uncomfortably but she was determined to finish. "I've never been so glad to see anyone in my life and I want you to know that I'm grateful."

"Forget it," he snapped. "I'm sure you'd have done the same thing for me if the situations were reversed." His tanned face softened and he touched her cheek with one lean finger. "I shouldn't have yelled at you like I did. It gave me quite a scare to see you lying there so still with him about to hit you. I thought you were either dead or unconscious." He shrugged. "And maybe it hurt my ego a bit to realize that it hadn't even occurred to you to call for help." He smiled at her with rueful apology.

Neither of them had a watch so there was no way of keeping an accurate account of the passing hours. A watch had been the least of Bree's concerns when she had dressed under the watchful eyes of the terrorists and Sean said he never wore one when he went camping, preferring to leave behind such a potent reminder of civilization. Bree guessed that it was about nine o'clock in the morning when they started out. Sean thought that with luck they should be able to walk out of the canyon in three or four days. It would have been much faster if they could have walked along the road, maybe hitching a ride with a passing motorist, but they didn't dare risk it. The terrorists

47

were bound to be watching the road carefully, so it was best that Bree and Sean avoid it. Hiking through the woods above the road would slow them, but it was safer.

Bree wondered if perhaps she was callous to be unable to feel any real regret at the death of the kidnapper, but then she dismissed the thought. She did not rejoice in his death, but it had been a case of his life or hers and she couldn't pretend to be sorry that she was the one who was alive.

She watched Sean's broad back as he walked ahead of her and marveled at the fact that she had known him less than forty-eight hours and yet he had just killed a man in her defense. The thought sent a primitive thrill coursing through her. She could not suppress the feeling that she belonged to him in some way. She scoffed at the idea. But the feeling persisted. It was just gratitude, she told herself. *You're blowing simple gratitude all out of proportion.* But she knew it wasn't that. He had saved her from certain rape and almost as certainly an unpleasant death. She was grateful. Very grateful! But there was more to what she was feeling than just gratitude. She felt . . . branded, as if he had marked her as his and, to her amazement, the sensation was not at all disagreeable. That discovery was more disconcerting than anything else. She had always been a very independent person, not at all the kind of woman to enjoy the feeling of being owned by a man and yet, here she was, admitting to a feeling of pleasure at the thought of belonging to a man she had known for scarcely two days. Maybe she'd been out in the sun too long.

She considered what she knew of the man ahead of her and had to admit that it wasn't much. He was in some line of work in which he habitually wore a gun. She had already speculated on the possibilities that came to mind, but she was not any closer to knowing what he did for a living and his evasiveness made it clear that he wasn't any too eager to volunteer information. She estimated his age to somewhere around forty, and he exuded the kind of natural authority that she had seen only in men who were in command, so he was probably in charge of something. But of what, she had no idea. She had had no doubts about his ability to take care of himself even before his swift handling of the terrorist who had attacked her. He looked and moved like a man in superb physical condition.

She allowed her eyes to dwell thoughtfully on what she could see of his back. His pack concealed most of it, but she could fill in the missing pieces from memory. She wondered what he would look like without a shirt. Probably devastating. She became aware of the direction her thoughts were drifting and she jerked her eyes away, focusing them on the path they were following. Good heavens! She was practically drooling over the man. She had definitely been out in the sun too long!

49

CHAPTER FOUR

It seemed like she had spent her entire life on her feet by the time they stopped for lunch. She wondered how Sean managed to look so alert when she felt like collapsing in a heap. The man obviously wasn't human. He told her to sit down and relax but she knew that he must be just as tired as she was, if not more so, and she helped him gather together some dry twigs and pine needles to start a small fire. Once the fire was started he dug through his pack and came up with a small pan and some packages of dehydrated soup. Bree couldn't help but smile. A few days ago a cup of dehydrated vegetable soup with some beef jerky shredded into it would not have been her idea of a gourmet feast and yet, right now, she couldn't imagine anything that would taste more heavenly.

"What do you do when you're not being kidnaped by terrorists?" Sean grinned over at her and she was struck again by his sheer sexual magnetism.

She took another sip of soup before answering his question. With only one mug between them, he had insisted that she use it while he ate out of the pan and he looked amazingly primitive sitting cross-legged across the fire from her, his shirt partially unbuttoned and a three-day growth of beard darkening his jaw.

"Oh, I only get kidnaped on Tuesdays. The rest of the time I'm a photographer. Mostly wildlife, but I've also done some work with children. I wish I had my camera right now," she added absently. "You look like something straight out of the Wild West."

His brows rose in amusement and he looked her over critically. "Well, I'd like to be able to say that you look like a prairie blossom but, to tell the truth, you look more like Jesse James's sidekick." She finished the last of her soup and eyed him consideringly.

"The way you look right now would make even Jesse James take flight. That beard gives you a very piratical air."

He rubbed a hand over his whiskers and grimaced at the rasping feel of them. "Tomorrow morning I'm going to shave even if there's a whole army of terrorists lurking in the bushes. But enough about my disreputable appearance. How did you get into wildlife photography?"

She leaned back against a tree trunk and stretched her legs out in front of her, noticing absently that there was a large tear in one leg of her jeans. "Well, Dad was an ambassador before he became a senator and he was stationed in a number of different countries while I was growing up. He used to take me out hiking with him whenever he could get away and when he didn't have the time I'd go with my brother, so I got to see a lot of wild country when I was young. I always loved it and I couldn't imagine myself ever being happy tied to a desk job, so I started looking around for a way that I could earn a living by spending my time in the great outdoors.

"My parents bought me a camera for my tenth birthday and I took pictures of everything that moved and of quite a few things that didn't. Just for fun Dad sent some of my pictures into a magazine contest when I was about twelve. They didn't win the contest, but the publishers wanted to buy them to use with an article they had in the works."

She smiled reminiscently. "I was so excited, I could hardly breathe and I decided right then that I wanted to be a professional photographer."

"Do you free-lance or work for somebody in particular?"

"A little of both. I do a lot of work for a wildlife magazine, but I free-lance too. I love it. I've traveled all over the world." She laughed. "Mark always protests that it's dangerous and that one of these days I'm going to get in trouble. My last assignment was in South America and he squawked about it being politically unstable. He was sure I was going to get shot or eaten by a crocodile. I didn't have any problems there, but I came home just in time to get kidnaped out of my own bed. I'll have to point that out to him the next time he fusses about a trip."

Sean watched the play of emotions over her face as she talked, marveling that she could laugh and joke as if she hadn't just undergone an ordeal that would have reduced most people to silence, if not hysterics. She certainly was a gutsy woman. Beautiful, too, he thought, noticing the way the sun highlighted the fire in her hair. His brows drew into a faint frown as she mentioned Mark again. Who was Mark and what was he to her? Of course it was none of his business, but he couldn't help but wonder and, he admitted to himself, he couldn't deny a faint twinge of jealousy at the easy way she spoke the other man's name. The sooner he got her back to Denver and out of his sight, the better, he told himself firmly. The last thing he needed or wanted was to become involved with a woman half his age.

After a brief break for lunch they moved on again. Conversation was nonexistent between them now. It was too much trouble to talk and watch the trail at the same time and, by mid-afternoon, they were both too tired to have the energy to converse even if it had been convenient.

Sean called a halt just before dusk. Bree was already half asleep on her feet but she helped him gather together a large pile of pine needles on which he spread out his sleeping bag. He didn't want to risk lighting a fire, fearing that the light might act as a beacon for anyone still searching for them, so they made a meal out of beef jerky and a handful of dried fruit each, washed down with water from his canteen. It was an adequate if dull meal since they were both too tired to be really hungry.

Bree shivered in the late fall chill and it suddenly occurred to her to wonder what kind of sleeping arrangements he had in mind. It was obviously going to get too cold for either of them to sleep on the ground, but it was going to be mighty crowded with the two of them in a sleeping bag together.

He caught her dubious look in the last waning daylight and his mouth twisted in a half smile. "It's too cold for either of us to sleep without a blanket," he said, echoing her own thoughts. "It's a big sleeping bag and, quite frankly, I'm too tired to be dangerous."

Bree hesitated for only a moment, made uncertain more because of her own reactions to him than because she thought he was likely to make a pass at her. But he was right; they really didn't have any choice and she gave him a tired grin.

"I hope you don't snore."

She tugged off her boots and slipped her belt off before climbing into the sleeping bag. He was right—it was a big bag, more than big enough for her alone, but it was going to be just a little crowded with the two of them. Oh, well, shared body heat was one of the best ways to avoid freezing to death in the wilderness, she reminded herself.

She heard him rustling around. Presumably he was also removing his boots and belt. And then she felt a draft as he pulled open the top of the bag and slid in next to her. She stiffened involuntarily at the warm brush of him. She lay facing away from the center of the bag, her back rigid as she tried to avoid coming into contact with him.

There was a brief sigh from Sean and then he had taken hold of her shoulder and was turning her firmly around until she was facing him. "I told you, I'm too tired to be dangerous. Now, why don't you get comfortable and we'll both try to get some sleep."

With his arm under her neck, her head fell naturally onto the pillow of his shoulder and, with a tired sigh, she relaxed against him. Within minutes she was sound asleep, her body cuddled up against his comfortably. Sean felt her soft warmth and the tickle of her hair against his chin and thought ruefully that maybe he wasn't as tired as he had thought.

His body craved sleep but his mind was still active, and he settled her more closely against him and allowed his thoughts to wander. He was fairly sure that they had seen the last of the terrorists. Unless they were absolute fools, they would cut their losses and try to get out of the country. They must have found the body of their compatriot by now and they would realize that Bree was no longer alone. Of course, there was no telling what men like that would do. He had dealt with their kind in too many places to make the mistake of thinking that they were predictable. That's what made them so dangerous, their unpredictability. But even if they were still looking for Bree, the chances of their finding them were fairly small. It wasn't likely that they had a skilled tracker with them and he had deliberately laid a trail across areas that would be difficult to follow. He doubted if Bree had even been aware of how often they had detoured from the direct route to walk across rock outcroppings.

He slid his hand across her back. Such a fragile-feeling creature and yet she had kept up with him without complaint, never asking to stop to rest. He knew that she was stiff and sore and yet she had laughed off her bruises. She had a kind of courage that he had seldom seen, even among men he had fought beside. And she had a strong sense of privacy, her own as well as others. He was not unaware of her curiosity about him, but she had never stepped beyond the bounds of polite curiosity into plain nosiness. All in all, she was quite a woman. Too young for him, of course, but quite a woman nonetheless. His last conscious thought was to wonder who Mark was and if he appreciated her.

Bree came awake slowly the next morning, conscious of feeling safe and warm even before she opened her eyes. During the night she had cuddled up closer to the man at her side, her leg thrown across his thighs and one arm laid across his broad chest. She could tell by his deep, even breathing that he was still asleep and she opened her eyes slowly, not moving from her comfortable position. Her view was restricted to an expanse of flannel-covered chest and she admired its muscular breadth somewhat absently.

He was really the most remarkable man she had ever met. Most men of her acquaintance would have been lost in a similar situation and she knew that she would have had to take care of them as well as herself, just as she had thought she would have to when she had first stumbled over Sean. Her mouth tilted in a smile as she remembered her irritation at having to take care of a tourist. Instead, he had been the one to take care of her and, though she hated to admit it, she wasn't sure that she could have made it this far without him.

The first few buttons on his shirt were undone and she idly slid her hand inside the opening, curling her fingers gently into the hair-rough skin of his chest. She was hardly aware of her actions until his hand, which had been resting on her shoulder, moved to slide under her chin, drawing her face up to his. His eyes were half closed as they swept over her face in a look that made her breath catch in her throat and her nails flex against his skin. She caught his gaze and he stifled a groan as her tongue came out to moisten lips that had suddenly gone dry.

His hand tightened on her chin an instant before his lips claimed hers with devastating force. There was no need for any tentative preliminary forays between them. Passion flared instantly. Her lips parted easily to admit him and her tongue engaged his in a primitive battle for supremacy that neither of them wanted or needed to win.

The arm that had been beneath her back tightened to bring her body more firmly against his, but even that was not enough to satisfy him and she murmured her approval when he shifted their positions until she lay flat on her back, the hard wall of his chest crushing her breasts as he leaned over her. Her breathing was as ragged as his when the kiss ended. Her arms slid around his back, her fingers molding the muscles there.

She almost purred with pleasure when his lips trailed across her cheek to her ear. His tongue traced its delicate convolutions before his teeth sank into the fleshy lobe. She felt his muscles harden at her throaty murmur and there was a raging passion in the lips that claimed hers.

The sleeping bag formed a warm cocoon around them, insulating them from the outside world and enveloping them in a private one of their own. Bree's senses seemed to be tuned to a fine pitch and she was acutely aware of the taste and texture of the man above her. His shirt had come unbuttoned the rest of the way and she slid her hands underneath it, running them up and down the smooth warmth of his back. The harsh rasp of his beard against her soft skin was an added stimulant to her already sensitized nerve endings.

The buttons of both her shirts were easily dispensed with and Bree bit her lip to stifle a cry of pleasure as his hand slid across the nylon pajama top to cup her breast. His thumb circled her nipple, brushing back and forth over the tender peak until it hardened into an aching point. She arched up against him until her thighs were molded to his lean hips and she could feel every taut muscle there. With a muffled groan Sean dragged his hand away from her breast to clasp her hip, forcing her away from him as he broke off their kiss.

"No!"

Bree was so caught up in the throbbing need he had aroused in her that it was a moment before she heard his strangled protest. Her eyes fluttered open to meet the almost black of his and she felt the shudder that went through him as he read the open desire in hers. Her hands slid up to his shoulders and she tried to pull him back down to her, but he resisted her urging until she gave up trying to move him.

"What's wrong?" she asked huskily.

He pulled out of her hold and reached across her to unzip the sleeping bag, throwing back the top layer and letting the morning air in to cool their overheated bodies.

Bree shivered and pulled the outer flannel shirt closed as she watched him get up and stand with his back to her. She stood up, too, and reached out a tentative hand to touch his shoulder, surprised by the rigid tension of the muscles there.

"Sean? What is it? Is it something I did?"

He turned and gave her a strained smile, his eyes flickering over her dishevelment before meeting hers. "It's nothing you did. There's just something about you that makes me lose control."

She stepped closer and laid her palm flat against his bare chest, her eyes meeting his openly. "Why should you worry about it? Maybe I'd like it if you'd lose control. I wasn't exactly kicking and screaming, you know."

His lips twisted in a reluctant smile. "I seem to recall that you're not all that big on kicking and screaming under any circumstances, but that's not the reason I stopped." He stepped back from her and she let her hand drop to her side as he began to button his shirt. "The point is that this isn't the right time or place to start something we might not be ready for. Wait till I get you back to civilization and then I'll abandon all my scruples about your maidenly virtue."

She couldn't help but smile at his leering grin, but she was conscious of an unfulfilled ache in her body that she had a feeling wasn't going to go away quickly.

CHAPTER FIVE

They were traveling across a slope that was only lightly forested, allowing them to walk side by side, and Bree stole occasional glances at the man next to her. He had had his promised shave this morning, using water heated over a small fire, old-fashioned shaving soap, and a straight razor. The result was really not at all fair, she thought. He had been attractive with several days growth of beard, but clean-shaven he was devastating. He had lost some of his piratical air, but it had been replaced by a look of rugged attractiveness that reminded her of the men who posed for cigarette commercials. It was all too easy to picture him rounding up cattle or having a shootout with rustlers.

She shook off the fancy and half-grinned to herself. He might look the part but she just couldn't quite imagine him modeling. He was much too elemental for that.

"Where were you born?"

He glanced at her, surprised, but his answer came easily. "California. Why?"

She shrugged. "No particular reason. Just curious. Are you an only child?"

"No. I have two younger brothers, both of them still in California."

The idea of his having brothers was somehow surprising. He seemed so independent and self-sufficient that it was hard for her to imagine him as a child, let alone with a family. Good Lord! Maybe he was married! He could have a whole slew of children of his own for all she knew. The thought brought a surge of pain that frightened her. Why should it matter to her if he were married? She found him attractive but it was no crime to think a married man was attractive.

She glanced up, startled out of her reverie as Sean came to a halt, putting out his hand to stop her from walking blindly into the stream they had come to. It was a large stream, not quite big enough to be called a river. Upstream it rushed over its stony bed with a soft sound but right in front of them, it widened out to form a deep, still pool.

Looking at the sun-dappled water, Bree was suddenly conscious of her griminess and she looked longingly at the pool.

"I don't suppose we could pause long enough to take a bath? I feel like a prisoner in the Bastille must have after a year or two with no water to wash with."

Sean chuckled at her wistful tone and started to shrug off his pack. "It'll be cold," he warned her as he knelt to pull things out of the pack.

"I don't care if it's pure ice. If I don't get clean, I'm going to go completely crazy."

"Well, if you promise to be good and not stay in the water too long and catch a chill, I might be persuaded to let you have some of my soap." As he spoke he pulled out a bar of soap and two small bath towels. Bree eyed the small green rectangle covetously.

"The way I feel right now you're taking your life in your hands to even imply that you might try to horde the soap. Any court would rule it justifiable homicide if I murdered you for possession of it."

Sean laughed and broke the bar in two pieces, giving her

the bigger piece. He spread out his sleeping bag before getting to his feet and handing her a towel. "We can have lunch on the sleeping bag when you're done. "I'll go downstream and wash up myself. Don't stay in too long and watch your footing. The rocks are bound to be slippery. All right, I'm going," he said as she gestured impatiently with one hand, anxious for him to go away so that she could get into the lovely water.

He was barely out of sight before she began tugging impatiently at her buttons and, a few minutes later, she stood naked under the sun. The late fall weather was cool but not cold and she reveled in the feel of the clean breeze across her body before she waded into the water until she was waist deep. It was, as Sean had warned, cold, but it wasn't freezing and, after the first shock, she found the brisk temperature invigorating. She took heed of his warning not to get chilled and began to soap herself briskly. She hesitated for only an instant before ducking her head under and then soaping up her hair. Maybe it wasn't the smart thing to do, but she really couldn't stand to leave it dirty.

When she stepped up onto the grassy bank, she felt like a new woman. Never again would she take for granted the simple pleasure of being clean. She shivered as the cool breeze hit her damp body and she quickly dried herself with the towel Sean had left her before wrapping it around her hair in a turban. She grimaced at the thought of putting her dirty clothes back on over her clean body, but it was too cold to stand around naked so she moved over to where they lay and reached down to pick up her pajama top. She picked up the handful of nylon and then stumbled backward, a startled scream leaving her throat to pierce the mountain quiet.

Perched solidly on top of her remaining clothes was a very large brown spider who seemed to be waving his legs at her in a threatening manner. Spiders were her only phobia. She had tried time and again to get over her fear, but the sight of a small house spider was enough to make her break out in a cold sweat. And this was definitely not a small house spider. To her terrified eyes he looked big enough for inclusion in a horror movie without the need for additional special effects. She backed slowly away from him, barely aware of a loud crashing noise until Sean burst into sight.

At another time she might have been struck by the picture he made as he stood framed by the dark green of the pine trees behind him. His hair was damp and tousled, falling into a deep wave across his forehead. He was wearing his jeans, zipped but not buttoned, and his chest was bare. He had on socks but no shoes. In his right hand was his pistol and in his left was the holster he had jerked it out of. He looked wildly around, expecting to find her under attack.

When he saw no sign of a terrorist he relaxed only slightly. "What's wrong?"

Bree could not find a voice to answer him and she pointed with one trembling hand to her clothes. Her other hand clutched the nylon pajama top in front of her as a wholly inadequate covering. Sean looked to where she pointed but could see no sign of anything dangerous. Bree managed to get out one shaken word.

"Spider!"

His brows jerked up and then drew together in an incredulous frown. He moved over to her clothes, expecting to see a six-pound black widow at the very least and finding nothing but an ordinary brown spider. He shoved his gun back in the holster and turned to Bree.

"You screamed like that because of a spider?"

She nodded, feeling somewhat foolish now that she was over her first fright. "Do you mean to tell me that a woman who gets kidnaped, escapes, knocks out one of her kidnapers, and endures an attack by another in stoic silence, a woman who experiences all that without so much as a whimper screams at the sight of a little spider?"

Bree scowled at him and tightened her grip on the top. "You needn't make a production out of it! I was startled, that's all!"

"That's all! Woman, I thought you were being murdered!" His eyes began to crinkle with laughter. "And all it was was a little spider."

"It's not funny!" she said angrily. She could see that he was making a valiant attempt to stay sober, but the humor of the situation was too much for him and he began to laugh uproariously. She glared at him furiously, barely restraining the urge to stamp her foot in childish rage. How dare he laugh at her! "Stop it!" He gasped and tried, but the waves of laughter would not be stopped. With an enraged snarl Bree dropped her frail covering, abandoning all thoughts of modesty, and launched herself at him.

Sean staggered back under her attack, still shaking with laughter as he tried to get a grip on her arms as she pounded him with her fists. Bree was strong for her size but it took him only a moment to subdue her by simply wrapping his arms around her and pulling her wiggling form against his body. She struggled furiously, her anger fueled by the tremors of laughter that still shook the broad chest beneath her trapped hands.

"Stop it, you little wildcat! I'm sorry I laughed." But his

apology was spoiled by the amusement that laced his voice and Bree growled with impotent rage as she fought to get just one hand loose to punish him with. It only made her angrier when she realized that he didn't seem to be exerting any effort to hold her, while she was panting with exertion.

"Let me go, damn you!" she ordered fiercely.

"I'm not going to let you go until you calm down. If I turn you loose now, you'd do your best to murder me."

Bree didn't bother to deny it. She had managed to hook her foot around his knee and, with a murderous smile, she jerked with all her strength, sure that he would have to let her go to save himself from falling. She should have known better. She heard his startled grunt as her action threw him off-balance, but instead of releasing her he tightened his grip as he began to fall, turning to the side so that his shoulder would take the brunt of the fall.

It was over in a matter of seconds and Bree opened her eyes, which she had squeezed shut when she felt herself falling, to look up into his face. He had rolled over as soon as they hit the ground so that now she lay pinned beneath him. She was suddenly aware of her nudity as she felt the firm warmth of his chest against her bare breasts. Her hands were pinned by his on either side of her head and she realized vaguely that they must have fallen onto his sleeping bag.

Her anger was gone as quickly as it had risen and she stared up at him wide-eyed, all too aware that every shaken breath she took pressed her breasts more firmly against his chest. His awareness of her was written in the lambent flames that began to burn in his eyes.

"Hellcat." She heard his soft murmur only an instant before his mouth touched hers. The fires they had lit earlier had died down to smoldering coals that took only a breath of passion to flare up. His lips took hers with a soft violence that told her of his need, his tongue thrusting aggressively between her teeth to explore the warm cavern of her mouth. Bree arched her body upward, enjoying the exciting roughness of his jeans against her thighs.

She barely noticed when he released her hands; she only knew that they were free to touch him as she longed to. She gripped his shoulders, her fingers flexing as she reveled in the taste and scent of him. The herbal scent of his soap clung to his skin—or was that the scent that lingered on her skin? No matter, it was difficult to tell where one began and the other ended. They seemed to flow into each other until they were one entity.

Sean dragged his mouth away from hers and blazed a fiery path down the taut curve of her neck to the pulse that pounded betrayingly at its base. His tongue probed the hollow there until he had elicited a gasp of pleasure from her before continuing the journey to the upper curves of her breasts. Bree closed her eyes against the dappled sunlight, not wanting it to intrude on her now.

She heard his sharp intake of breath and knew he must have seen the bruises that marked the pale flesh. "I should have killed all of them," he muttered harshly. Later she might wonder at the fierceness of his anger, but right now she was concerned with other things.

Sean's lips and tongue traced a teasing pattern around her breast, tasting every curve until Bree moaned aloud in frustration. When he began to do the same to its mate, she buried her hands in his hair, forcing his head down. She heard his husky laugh a moment before his mouth encircled her taut nipple and she purred with satisfaction as he suckled at the pink bud and then used his teeth to tug on it gently.

Her hands left his shoulders to slide restlessly down his back, her fingers tracing the length of his spine until they encountered his jeans and then slipping just inside the waistband and sliding around the cloth to meet in the front. She felt his stomach muscles contract at the intimate contact and she fumbled with his zipper, suddenly impatient with this last barrier between them. In a moment he was free of the garment and Bree gasped as he settled back down against her, evidence of his arousal hard and warm against her smooth stomach.

His mouth abandoned her throbbing breasts to recapture her lips as his hands began a sensual exploration of their own. They cupped the full warmth of her breasts, kneading them with an expertise that left her gasping before they slid down the smooth line of her belly to mold and shape her hips. His hair-rough thigh slid firmly between hers and she heard his low growl of satisfaction as she arched in involuntary response to the invasion. His hands moved to part her legs still farther and then his fingers were tracing a wild pattern up the inside of her thighs until she grew taut as a bow string waiting for his next touch.

"Oh!" she shuddered as he finally reached his goal and his hand closed over her.

"So soft and warm for me," he murmured next to her ear as his fingers began an intimate exploration that made her whimper with pleasure. "Oh, God, Bree! I can't stand much more. I want you so badly!"

"Now, Sean! Please, now!" Her husky plea broke the last remnants of his control and his hands gripped her hips as he moved over her. She opened her eyes and looked into the fierce warmth of his as he supported himself above her. At that moment she realized that she was falling in love with this man. It didn't matter that she didn't know anything about him or that she had met him less than forty-eight hours ago. She loved him, pure and simple. The knowledge added an extra urgency to her response and she arched beneath him, begging him to complete the embrace.

He surged against her almost violently, filling the aching void with his warmth, his mouth smothering her half-uttered cry of fulfillment. She felt the shudder that went through his frame and knew a sense of triumph that he was affected as strongly as herself. He began to move, slowly at first, gradually increasing the rhythm as he felt her instant response to his slightest move.

Bree was caught up in the rhythm he set, her body trembling beneath his thrusting weight. She buried her face against his shoulder, her teeth inflicting a sensuous pain on the rippling muscles there. A fine film of perspiration coated them both, welding them more closely together. Her breath came in deep gulps as the tension in her body began to heighten, gathering inside her until she thought she would surely die if it didn't break.

Sean felt the shivering in her begin and he thrust deeply, drawing his head back until he could see her face as the tension within her snapped into an explosion of pleasure. Her eyes widened endlessly and she let herself fall into the deep pool of sensation that opened for her. Her nails dug into his back as she arched against him and he gave a shuddering groan as he released his control.

It seemed like a lifetime before either of them felt capable of moving. With an effort Sean rolled to the side, his arm hooking around her waist to keep her close against him. He buried his face in her tousled curls, still damp from her makeshift bath. Bree curled herself into the curve of his body, her head resting naturally on his shoulder.

"You smell nice, like an herb garden," he murmured into her damp hair. His hands stroked gently across her back.

"You say that only because it's your soap that makes me smell like that."

"I didn't plan on this happening, you know."

There was a suggestion of anxiety in his tone and she smiled without opening her eyes, curling her fingertips gently into the hair on his chest. "I didn't think you planted that spider on my clothes."

"That's another thing. If you're really afraid of spiders, I shouldn't have laughed. Everyone has their weak spots."

Bree opened her eyes and shifted her position to lean on one elbow next to him, her breasts brushing tantalizingly across his chest as she looked down at him. She could not resist the urge to push his tousled hair back off his forehead, and she smiled down at him.

"Are you going to apologize for making love to me? Because if you are, I should warn you that I would probably be forced to do my best to drown you in the stream." She saw the gleam of laughter that lit his dark eyes and her smile broadened. "I suppose you think I couldn't do it after my recent display, but you were only able to overcome me so easily because I was angry. Anger always makes me weak. Mark keeps lecturing me on learning to control my temper but, so far, with only limited results. What's wrong?" Sean rolled to one side and sat up, presenting Bree with an uncompromising view of his taut, muscled back.

Bree barely held back a gasp of shock. Where on earth had he gotten that scar? It started under his shoulder blade and ran in a jagged, curving line down his back before it disappeared around his side. She almost reached out to touch the whitened flesh, but something in the rigid line of his back stopped her.

"Sean? What's wrong?"

His shoulders tensed as if her question were a lash laid across them, and she rose to her knees behind him, suddenly aware of the cool breeze that was blowing across the clearing. He reached for his hastily discarded jeans and got to his feet to pull them on. Bree watched him silently, hurt confusion easily read in her face, but Sean didn't look at her as he spoke.

"Nothing's wrong. Let's just say that what just happened shouldn't have. This really isn't the time or . . ."

"The place," she finished acidly. "If you tell me that one more time, I swear I'll shoot you!" She got to her feet and strode angrily to where her clothes lay. She snatched them up, uncaring of any possible spiders that might be lurking there. The way she felt right now she could have taken on an entire army of spiders.

Sean could not help but admire her long-legged beauty, graceful even in anger. In her jeans and shapeless shirts it had been difficult to see her figure and a few minutes ago he had had other things on his mind besides an analytical appraisal of her body, but now he couldn't tear his eyes away as she began to dress. Her hair was almost dry and it fell in burnished disarray against her shoulders, making him itch to run his fingers through it. Her breasts were firm and well-shaped, just the size to fill a man's hands.

He followed the smooth, tapering line of her stomach to the flare of her thighs. Bree would have told him that her hips were too broad, but he could find nothing to criticize in them. He clenched his hands into tight fists, angry that he should torture himself like this. But he couldn't forget the softness of her mouth or the feel of her body arching up to meet the thrusting hardness of his.

Bree finished buttoning her shirt slowly, then drew his flannel shirt over it, well aware of his dark eyes watching her every move. She turned to face him, her gaze flickering over him, and she barely restrained a malicious grin as she took in his obvious arousal. Normally she would have been filled with contempt by a woman who teased but she didn't feel even a flicker of guilt. She hadn't asked him to watch her dress; he had chosen to do so and it served him right if he was suffering now. He had taken what should have been a beautiful moment of love between them and made it seem cheap and tawdry, and she resented it.

Her eyes met his with deliberate insolence. "I seem to have lost my appetite for lunch. Why don't we put a few more miles behind us, if you don't mind."

It was easy for Sean to read the expression in her sapphire eyes and he ground his teeth together angrily before forcing himself to relax. If he looked at things from her point of view, he could see how she might feel that she had a right to be angry. He couldn't blame her for a desire to punish him.

Bree was almost sorry when the anger faded from his eyes and he nodded agreement. "Let me go get my shirt and boots and I'll be right with you."

When he was gone she stalked angrily about for a minute, blind to the peaceful beauty of her surroundings. How dare he make her feel cheap? And how dare he turn his back on a fight when she was spoiling to have one? She knelt by his sleeping bag and began to roll it up with short, jerky movements, forcing her mind away from what had occurred there a short while ago. The sooner she got home to Denver, the better.

CHAPTER SIX

Though the area they were walking through was open enough to allow them to walk together, Bree chose to walk a few paces behind Sean. It was not that she was sulking, she told herself. It was just that she didn't trust herself not to push him off a cliff if she got the chance. She would have been among the first to admit that her temper was a little too quick. Over the years she had learned to control it for the most part and she had always been proud of the fact that while she might anger easily, she never carried a grudge. This was one time, however, when she was definitely working up to a grudge.

She glared at the masculine back in front of her, thinking dark thoughts of torture and murder. He was a pompous, overbearing, egotistical male and she must have been demented to have thought that she could possibly be in love with him. The sooner she could get home, the sooner she could forget all about him. She would write the entire, unfortunate incident off as a temporary delusion on her part. Somewhere deep inside she knew that she was deliberately whipping up her anger because she was afraid that if she didn't have anger to use as a shield, she might fall completely apart and break down and cry.

They were crossing a broad rock ledge above a shale slope when a horrifying thought assailed her. My God! What about tonight? Where was she going to sleep? One thing was certain—she was not about to share a sleeping bag with him no matter how cold it got!

Distracted by her thoughts, she put her foot down carelessly. She felt the sharp stab of a stone through the soft suede sole of her boot. With a small gasp of pain she jerked her foot back up just as her other foot began to slip on the loose stones that littered the ledge.

Sean, alerted perhaps by a small sound or maybe by some sixth sense, spun around just in time to see her lose her balance and fall toward the slope. He lunged toward her in a desperate effort to stop her fall, but his fingertips just brushed the leg of her pants as she slid off the solid rock ledge and onto the shale below. He saw her throw her arms over her face as she began to roll, but he was already tearing at the chest strap of his pack. He jerked the pack off and let it fall next to the rifle she had dropped and then started down the slope at a plunging run, angling his descent toward her.

It seemed like she would never stop her rolling fall and he half-slid, half-fell in an effort to get beneath her and stop her. At the bottom of the slope was a cliff of fifteen feet or so, more than enough to break several bones if she fell off it. She had rolled perhaps seventy-five feet when she was stopped by the remains of a lightning-blasted tree. She slammed into the barrier with enough force to cause the weakened trunk to crack ominously, but it held, and seconds later Sean reached her still form.

She lay on her back, her arms at her sides, and for a frantic moment he could detect no sign of breathing. When she took a gasping breath he realized that she must have had the wind knocked out of her by her collision with the stump. He ran his hands over her body, breathing a cautious sigh of relief when he found no sign of broken bones, but he winced at the sight of her forearms. The flannel shirt was shredded from contact with the sharp stone and the red plaid was now stained with the darker tint of blood, but he couldn't really tell how badly she was hurt until he could wash away the dirt and blood. He frowned as he looked back up the slope to where his pack lay and then back to Bree.

"Bree? Can you hear me?" He leaned close and spoke loudly. "Bree?"

Her eyes opened and she stared up at him blankly, her eyes gradually focusing on him. She wet her lips and he had to strain his ears to hear her. "Watch out for that first step. It's a doozy." Her eyes began to drift shut as if that small effort had exhausted her.

"Bree!" He said her name urgently. "Honey, you've got to help me get you up. Do you understand? I'm going to have to carry you back up the slope, but I need your help to get you over my shoulder. All right?"

Her lips moved again and he leaned close to catch her words. "Too heavy. Walk." He almost grinned.

"You can't be hurt too bad if you're already arguing with me, but you're in no condition to win a fight right now, so just do as I say. I'm going to get you onto your feet and then you can brace yourself against me while I get you over my shoulder. Can you do that? Bree! Answer me! You've got to stay conscious for just a few more seconds!"

"I'm awake," she told him in a cross mutter and then almost fainted as he began to pull her upright.

It seemed to take forever to get to the top of the slope that it had taken only seconds to get down. Bree was a dead weight across his shoulder and he assumed that she had lost consciousness. He hoped she had because the unavoidable jolting he was giving her would be agony if she were conscious. He lost track of the number of times the shale slipped treacherously beneath him, sending him to his knees. He concentrated all his energy on the five feet in front of him and, when that goal was reached, on the next five feet until he finally reached the top and staggered up onto the safety of the solid rock ledge. He was drenched in sweat from the exertion and he was afraid that if he put her down now, he wouldn't be able to pick her up again. They had passed an abandoned cabin about a quarter of a mile back. If he could get her to that, they would at least have some shelter when night fell.

He leaned down and got a grip on the rifle sling and the shoulder straps of his pack and then had to take a deep breath before he could stand upright with them in his hand. A faint whimper of pain reached him and he gritted his teeth before starting back the way they had come.

The cabin, when he got to it, was just as he remembered it from the brief look he had taken when they went by. Not too old, it was still in reasonably good repair. Probably originally built to be used as a hunting shack, the walls leaned a little drunkenly and the roof would undoubtedly leak when it rained, but right now it represented much-needed shelter. He turned the rusty handle on the door but had to put his free shoulder against it to force the warped panel open.

Once inside, he was pleased to see that it was reasonably clean. Dust lay thick on the crude table and the one rickety chair, but the boarded-up windows had served to keep animals from using it as a lair and a little dust never hurt anyone.

He dropped the pack and rifle on the wooden floor and shifted Bree off his shoulder and lowered her slowly to the floor, propping her against a wall while he jerked his pack open and pulled out his sleeping bag. Once it was unrolled on the floor, not too far from the stone fireplace, he lifted her and stretched her out on her back, flinching at the moan of pain that was torn from her lips.

"Bree?"

Her lids flickered open and she stared at him, her blue eyes darkened to almost black and blank with pain.

"I'm going to get some firewood and water. I'll be back in a few minutes and we'll see if you're really hurt or just making a play for sympathy." He didn't know if she even heard his small attempt at humor, but he thought there was a flicker of understanding in her eyes before she let them fall shut again.

By the simple expedient of sticking his head inside the fireplace and looking up the chimney he determined that whoever had built the cabin had had the foresight to cover the chimney with screening to prevent squirrels or birds from building nests in it. He had seldom seen such a lovely patch of clear blue sky as the small square that was framed by the stone walls of the chimney. It made things so much simpler to be able to use the fireplace.

A moment's scrounging in a corner turned up a battered but still serviceable pot. With another glance at Bree to make sure she hadn't moved, he ducked out the door and into the late afternoon sunshine. It took several trips to gather enough dead wood to last them through the night. When he felt that he had enough, he made his way to the tiny stream that trickled down the mountain not far from the cabin. A quick scrubbing with some river-bottom pebbles and the pot was clean, if not shiny, and he filled it with water before doing the same with his canteen.

Bree seemed to have lapsed into unconsciousness and Sean moved around quietly, building a fire and then hanging the kettle over it on the primitive but functional pot-hook that he found attached to the fireplace wall. Once the water was beginning to heat, he knelt by Bree's still figure and began unbuttoning her shirt. The first thing to do was to get her undressed and wash the dried blood and dirt off her arms and then he could begin to assess her injuries.

She came awake with a start to see the dark outline of a man kneeling above her, his hands removing the shirt, and her first thought was that she was with the kidnapers. With a stifled cry of fright she surged upward, batting futilely at his hands, knowing that she was too weak to fight him. Her sudden movement startled Sean, but he realized immediately that she was not really conscious and he easily avoided her weak blows to grasp her shoulders and force her gently but firmly back down on the sleeping bag.

"Bree, it's Sean! You're all right, honey. I've got you safe. Remember?" He spoke forcefully and his words penetrated the haze that surrounded her mind.

She blinked to clear her vision and looked up at him.

"I thought you were a terrorist. I should have realized that they don't come in large economy sizes. She relaxed. "Of course, I don't suppose you could be called an economy size. I bet it would cost a fortune to feed you." He frowned slightly and put his hand on her forehead and she managed a weak grin. "No, I'm not delirious. I'm just talking so I can forget how bad it hurts."

His frown didn't fade as he began to ease her out of her clothes. "Does anything feel broken?"

"Everything!" She winced as he slid the second tattered shirt off her shoulders, lifting her into a sitting position to do so. While he had her there he lifted her pajama top over her head. She eyed its battered condition with equanimity.

"I must say that I can't really grieve over its demise. I think I'd gotten a little tired of that shade of blue anyway." She obediently lifted her hips so that he could slide her jeans off, her eyes admiring his kneeling form with absent pleasure. "I suppose it's too late for a display of maidenly modesty." His lips twitched in a half grin at her philosophical tone.

"I'm afraid so." He ran his hands gently over her body, pausing when she winced, to check for serious injury. When he had completed his rough examination he sat back on his heels and gave her a relieved grin. "You'll live. No broken bones, but you may have cracked a rib when you hit that tree. As soon as the water boils and cools a bit, I'll be able to wash off the dirt and see about those cuts and scrapes."

"I wish you'd take off your shirt," she told him dreamily. "I bet you'd look magnificent crouched in the firelight." If it hadn't been dim in the little cabin and if she hadn't been hazy with pain, Bree might have noticed the faint tide of red that washed over his face.

"I thought you said you weren't delirious," he said gruffly.

"I'm not. Has anyone ever told you that you're a superb lover, Sean?"

"Not lately." He almost scalded his finger testing the water to see if it had cooled sufficiently.

"Well, I think it's about time somebody did. It's not fair that you should go unappreciated all these years, so I'll tell you right here and now that you're a superb lover."

"Why don't you just shut up and lay there like a proper invalid?" he growled.

Sean used a folded shirt as a potholder and pulled the pot off the fire. He poured some of the water from his canteen in to cool it until he could put his hand in it without burning himself, and then soaked a piece torn from one of his shirts in the water.

"This is going to be hot," he warned her before beginning the task of cleaning her arm. Aside from an initial gasp she made no sound during the entire procedure but Sean knew he had to be hurting her as he sponged away dirt, dried blood, and bits of stone. By the time he was done he had to control a fine tremor in his hands and there was sweat dripping off his forehead. He would rather have been the one who was injured than to have to deal with her pain. He strove to make his tone light when he spoke.

"You were lucky this time around. It's mostly just scrapes and bruises, painful but not fatal."

"That's great," she gasped. "I was afraid I wasn't going to make it there for a minute. I'm sorry, but I think I'm going to pass out." Her tone was faint but perfectly calm and it took Sean a minute to realize what she had said and by then, true to her word, she had quietly passed out.

Probably just as well, he thought. That way he could put antiseptic on her scrapes and cuts without worrying about hurting her anymore. Her arms had taken the brunt of the fall and they were marked with shallow cuts and scrapes. Her back appeared to be more bruised than scraped and her instinctive action of throwing her arms over her face had protected it from any damage at all. Darkness had fallen when he was done and he threw out the dirty water before shutting the warped door against the chill night air. Bree seemed to be resting quietly and he sat on the floor next to her, letting his eyes dwell on her face.

You're a fool, he thought. Only a fool would fall in love with a woman almost half his age and that was exactly what he had done. He had fallen passionately in love for the first time in his life and it had to be with a woman who was too young. He had known since the first time he kissed her that she could be trouble if he wasn't careful, and he had made up his mind to keep his emotions under control. Thrown together as they were, it would be all too easy to let things get out of hand between them.

His lips twisted in rueful acknowledgment of his own arrogance. He had been so sure that he could handle things and yet twice in twenty-four hours he had come close to losing his control. Once, when he had stepped into the little clearing above his car and found her being attacked. He still found it difficult to comprehend the sheer rage that had gripped him at that moment. He had been in life-and-death situations more times than he cared to remember and his presence here today was proof that he had always come out on top, but he had done so because of his ability to think coolly and clearly even under pressure. Yesterday he hadn't been thinking at all, and that worried him. When he had seen Bree in danger, he hadn't bothered to think; he had acted on instinct alone and that instinct had told him to kill. A primitive rage had filled his mind and he had seen the scruffy terrorist through a red haze. That creature had tried to harm his woman and Sean had reacted with blind instinct in defense of what was his.

With unaccustomed tenderness he leaned forward and brushed the burnished curls back off her forehead. She looked frighteningly young lying there and he grimaced again at his own foolishness. The second time he had come close to losing control had been this morning when he woke up with her in his sleeping bag. She had been so soft and desirable and willing that he had almost succumbed to the urge to make love to her. He had managed to hold on to his weakening resolve then, but this afternoon by the stream he had given up. Not that he could really claim to have lost control. He could have stopped; he had known that at the time, but he had admitted to himself that he didn't want to stop and he had selfishly taken what she so freely offered.

Bree stirred in her sleep and murmured something unintelligible in which only one word was clear. *Mark.* Sean's brows almost met in a sudden scowl and he turned to poke more wood into the fire with more force than was necessary. That was another thing. Who the hell was Mark, and what did he mean to her? He was probably some young puppy who couldn't possibly appreciate her. He sounded like a stuffed shirt. He didn't want her to go to South America because it might be dangerous. Well, so was crossing the street, but that didn't stop people from doing it. He thought she needed to control her temper. He probably wanted her to marry him and sit at home with nothing to do but take care of him. Fool! He'd never appreciate her for what she was. He'd try to make her into something else and destroy everything that made her such a unique and special woman.

With a sudden grin Sean realized what he was doing. He hadn't even met the man and he was already calling him names. For all he knew, Mark was a perfectly nice, respectable young man who would make a wonderful husband. But not for Bree, he added involuntarily. Damn! Why did he have to go and fall in love? He was too old for this kind of soul-searching.

Bree slept through the night, stirring restlessly once or twice and whimpering with pain but never coming fully awake. Sean leaned his back against the wall beside her and dozed fitfully, waking at her every move and checking anxiously for signs of fever.

She woke sometime after dawn. She knew it was morning by the sunshine that found its way between the cracks in the boarded-up windows. The stiffness of her body made her remember her fall with a faint shudder. She turned her head slightly until she could see her companion and her mouth tilted in a tender smile as she took in his slumped position. His head had fallen back against the wall and the dim light revealed the exhausted lines in his face with pitiless clarity. Her memories of the events immediately after her fall were hazy, but she remembered him carrying her for what had seemed like a long distance. No wonder he looked so tired. He must be absolutely exhausted.

She traced every feature with her eyes, admitting to herself that she had fallen deeply in love with him. He was a stranger in many ways. She knew virtually nothing about him, but it didn't matter. She loved him. She didn't care who he was or what he did for a living. For all she knew he was a criminal. She had to admit that the little she knew of him did not rule out this possibility, but she knew that criminal or not, he was an honorable man.

She shifted her position slightly and could not suppress a gasp of pain that even the small movement forced out of her. Sean was awake instantly, bending over her with a look of concern in his dark eyes that almost made her heart stop. He put his hand on her forehead and she saw relief on his face when he felt her cool skin.

"How are you feeling?" he asked softly.

Bree smiled up at him, touched by his tenderness. "It hurts only when I laugh."

"Then don't laugh," he murmured softly, bending his

head until his lips touched hers. He had intended it to be nothing more than a brief kiss to show her that he was glad she was all right, but, as always between them, as soon as their lips met, a spark flared up and Sean found himself hungry for more than just a brief touch. With an effort he drew back, the disturbed rhythm of his breathing a testament to his self-control. The hectic flush in her cheeks was not a sign of fever and he couldn't stifle a feeling of triumph over the fact that he could disturb her equilibrium so easily.

"If you weren't in such a weakened condition, I would be tempted to ravage your body," he told her huskily.

"I'll take that as a promise and I'll remind you of it when I can move again."

The next three days would have been idyllic if Bree hadn't been so stiff and sore. She had been very lucky to escape serious injury. Her wounds were, despite the discomfort they caused, basically superficial. They decided that she probably didn't have a cracked rib, but there was no way to be sure without an X ray and Sean apologetically admitted to having forgotten to bring the equipment for that. So her side turned every color of the rainbow but didn't cause her an excessive amount of pain and they just crossed their fingers and hoped it was nothing but a bad bruise. Her jeans had protected her legs from the rough shale and her arms had protected her face, but Sean's flannel shirt, her own shirt, and her pajama top had never been meant to take that kind of punishment and the material had shredded over her arms, leaving them bruised and cut. She was lucky to have gotten off as lightly as she had though it was a little difficult for her to fully appreciate that when she felt like she'd been run over by a steamroller. Sean nursed her carefully, feeding her and making sure her abrasions stayed clean.

She spent most of the first day after the fall dozing, waking up only briefly to let him feed her some of the inevitable soup before dropping off to sleep again. The next morning her body was still stiff and sore, but her mind was alert and she was already beginning to feel restless.

With nothing else to do they spent most of their time talking about anything and everything. A chance mention of a book she had read recently led to a discussion of the literary merits of various authors and Bree was amazed to discover that he was an avid reader like herself. Unthinkingly, she expressed her surprise and he grinned at her over the pot of soup he was heating.

"What's the matter? Didn't you think I could read?"

She blushed. "It's not that at all. It's just that I somehow never pictured you as the type to settle down with a good book."

He shrugged and her eyes were drawn to the bulging muscles of his shoulders, where they lingered appreciatively. "I've spent a lot of time in places where there were only two things to do with your free time—drink or read. I tried drinking for a while, but it got old fast so I settled on reading. I'll read just about anything I can get my hands on, but I lean toward some nice escapist science fiction."

Bree wrinkled her nose. "I've never been able to get into science fiction. If I have my choice, I like a good western with lots of shootouts."

"That just proves that you've got a plebeian imagination," he told her.

They argued amiably about any subject that came to

mind, but Bree found, to her frustration, that he revealed very little of his past unless questioned directly.

Two days after her fall she was watching him carefully cleaning his gun and a sudden thought popped into her head.

"Were you ever in the service?" she asked idly.

He stiffened and looked at her with a wary intensity that surprised her. "Why do you ask?"

Her brows rose at his almost hostile tone. "No particular reason. You're very efficient in an emergency and it just made her wonder."

His shoulders relaxed and he went back to cleaning the pistol, answering her with an ease that made her wonder if she had imagined his wariness. "I was in the marines twice. Once in fifty-eight and I joined again during Vietnam."

"My brother went to 'Nam" was her only comment, but she filed away this small tidbit of information. She knew so little about him.

Another time he happened to mention his brothers. "Are your brothers a lot younger than you?"

He shoved a few more branches into the fire, his eyes narrowing against the sudden flare of light. He thought for a moment before answering. "Richard must be thirty-nine now and David would be thirty-six."

"Are your parents still alive?" she asked softly.

"No. Dad was killed during the Korean War and Mom got pneumonia and died when I was nineteen."

"How terrible for you! What happened to your brothers? Did you have relatives to take them in?"

"Nope. We managed on our own." He got to his feet and stretched, making it clear that the conversation was over, but she ventured one more question.

"Do you see much of your brothers now?"

His eyelids came down, shuttering the expression in his eyes, and his voice was flat. "I haven't seen them in fifteen years."

Though she had only intended to ask one question, she was startled into asking, "Why?"

His massive shoulders lifted in a shrug. "Just haven't gotten around to going home." His expression made it clear that this time the subject was really closed.

Bree didn't probe any further, but she already had a lot to think about. She wasn't fooled by his casual statement that they had managed on their own after their mother's death. She had guessed his age at fortyish, so if he had been nineteen, then the two younger boys would have been eighteen and fifteen and three boys of that age did not manage easily. If they had managed, it must have meant a lot of hardships and she would bet that the bulk of the worry and hardship had fallen on Sean's shoulders. As the oldest and the only one out of school, he would have been the natural choice.

He must have joined the marines soon after his mother's death, maybe as a way to support his brothers, but they would still have been relatively young when his military stint was through. So what had he turned to then to support his family?

Bree shivered. Was that why he hadn't seen his brothers in fifteen years? Because he was a criminal? Why else would he be so cagy about his past? Had she fallen irrevocably in love with a criminal?

CHAPTER SEVEN

Four days after her fall Bree was beginning to get cabin fever. Though her muscles still protested her every move, they no longer screamed as loudly, and she was able to walk around the cabin without too much discomfort. Sean had gone out to do some exploring beyond their immediate vicinity. Though he was fairly certain that the terrorists must have given up the hunt by now, it would do no harm to make doubly sure that they weren't anywhere nearby.

He had left her with strict orders to take it easy, but the walls of the little cabin seemed to be closing in on her and with a guilty assurance to the absent Sean that she was just going to go a little way, Bree stepped out into the bright sunshine. She breathed deeply of the pine-scented air, feeling like a prisoner set free.

The early October weather was crisp and the air was crystal-clear. On a day like this it was difficult to remember her fright of a week ago when she had been kidnaped. The world seemed too beautiful a place for things like that to occur.

She walked around slowly, feeling some of the stiffness ease out of her muscles as she moved. She wandered down to the little stream that flowed just out of sight of the cabin and, on an impulse, she removed her jeans and pajama bottoms and knelt to wash them in the chill water. She hung them over a pine bough to dry in the light breeze and settled herself on a flat rock, leaning back on her elbows and letting the warmth of the sun ease the aches out of her bones. She stretched out her bare legs, noting absently the numerous bruises that covered them. Sean had given her one of his shirts to wear with a teasing warning to take better care of this one than she had of the last because it was the last one in his pack.

She had no idea how long she had been lying there when she heard her name called. She opened her eyes, startled to find that she had actually been dozing. A repeat of her name, this time with more urgency, brought her wide awake and she shouted an answer before easing herself into a sitting position on the rock.

Within seconds Sean strode into sight, his anxious expression changing to a thunderous scowl when he saw that she was all right.

"What do you think you're doing! I thought I told you to stay in the cabin!"

A few days ago she would have been infuriated by his tone, but after his tender care of her she couldn't help but feel that he had a right to scold her for worrying him. She gave him her most charming smile.

"I just couldn't resist getting out in the fresh air. I was very careful, honest. I didn't do anything foolish."

He relaxed and gave her a considering look. "You needn't think that I don't know what you're doing." She widened her blue eyes innocently at him and he gave her a reluctant grin. "Whoever taught you to use that smile like that deserves to be horsewhipped."

Bree didn't bother to dignify that with an answer. She just smiled at him guilelessly and held out her hand for him to help her down off her perch. He brushed it aside and put his hands around her waist, lifting her easily and setting her on the ground in front of him.

When he didn't release her Bree looked up at him, her eyes questioning, and she felt her breath catch at the expression on his face. "I don't suppose you're wearing anything under that shirt?" he asked huskily, his hands sliding up from her waist to rest just beneath the swell of her breasts.

Bree shook her head and swallowed hard, wondering if he could feel the sudden pounding of her heart. "I—I don't have anything to wear under it."

"That's what I was afraid you'd say." His head bent and his lips feathered across her eyes, sealing them shut before tracing a slow path to her ear. "Do you know what it does to me to know that you're almost naked?" She could feel his breath against her ear a moment before his teeth nipped gently at the fleshy lobe.

"What—what does it do to you?" she managed to ask, trying to hold on to her spinning senses as his tongue explored the area just beneath her ear with devastating results.

His hands slid to cup her buttocks and he lifted her up and against his thighs almost violently, telling her without words just what having her in his arms was doing to him. Her hands moved to grasp his shoulders and her head fell back in an open invitation, her arched neck offering an irresistible lure for his mouth. He explored every taut inch of her throat until Bree thought she would surely die from the sensations he was rousing in her. His hands continued to hold her pressed against his hardening thighs.

With a muttered oath he moved to swing her up into his arms. Bree's head fell naturally into the curve of his shoulder and she kept her eyes shut, not wanting anything, not even the gentle sunshine, to intrude on this moment.

She didn't open her eyes until he set her down, and she felt her bare feet touch the rough wood floor of the cabin. In the dim light he seemed to loom above her like a towering giant and she smiled tenderly and reached up to touch the silvery hair at his temples. His fingers worked the buttons on her shirt with barely controlled impatience and she shivered with pleasure when his hands finally slid inside to cup her breasts.

"Undress me," he ordered huskily. Her fingers went to the buttons on his shirt, but they were so weak that she fumbled awkwardly and when his thumbs brushed across her swollen nipples she could only gasp and cling to him helplessly. In the end she couldn't remember how his clothes got off; she could only remember her intense pleasure when at last her hands were free to roam over his muscled frame.

His large hand gripped the back of her head, tilting her face up to his and his mouth came down on hers. Their tongues met and entwined and then separated, only to meet again. Bree's hands moved frantically over him, her fingers rubbing through the hair on his chest before finding and touching the flat nipples hidden there. His sharp breath encouraged her and her exploration grew bolder as her fingers traced the line of hair down across his stomach, probed his navel, and then moved lower. Sean's breathing seemed to stop for a moment as she hesitated and then her hand closed firmly around him. He groaned against her mouth and his hands suddenly could not seem to get enough of her as they explored every inch of her willing body.

"Oh, God, Bree. I wanted this to last forever, but you're driving me crazy."

She was lowered gently onto the thick sleeping bag and his hard frame followed her down. His hips slid between her thighs and Bree almost purred her satisfaction when she felt his heat press against her. His mouth came down on hers and his tongue plunged into the moist warmth of her mouth at the same moment that he completed their union. He set up a primitive driving rhythm that seemed to touch her very core and Bree answered him with the demanding arch of her body. There was no time to savor their pleasure in each other as they surged together in a timeless rhythm. Sean felt her body go taut beneath him an instant before he reached his own peak. Her name was a hoarse groan against her throat as he shuddered in fulfillment.

After a long time he rolled to the side, careful to avoid her bruised and scratched arm and pulled her close into his side, letting her head fall onto his shoulder and his face rest against the soft cushion of her hair.

"I've never met a woman who could destroy my willpower the way you can. I promised myself that I wouldn't touch you again until I got you out of here, and you make me forget all about it without even trying."

"You don't regret it, do you?" She raised her head to ask him. He looked at her worried face and the uncertainty in her sapphire eyes and reached up a tender hand to smooth the tousled hair off her forehead. She felt the soft chuckle that reverberated in his chest a moment before he answered.

"Aren't I supposed to be asking you that? No, I don't regret it. How could I regret something so satisfying? I just hope you don't end up regretting it."

"Never!" she said fervently, and he smiled at her vehemence.

"Never is a very long time, sweetheart." He stilled her protest with a kiss.

They stayed in the little cabin for three more days and despite her battered condition, Bree had never been happier. By unspoken agreement neither of them mentioned the future or the past. As Bree's bruises began to fade Sean insisted that she take long walks to keep her muscles in good condition. While they walked they talked of impersonal things. Bree found that he was fully as well-traveled as she was and they discussed places they had both been and places they would like to see again.

Sean had found a battered deck of cards under an old box in one corner of the cabin and they played poker for astronomical stakes. By the end of their first evening of play Bree found herself owing Sean one million dollars. When he demanded that she pay up immediately, she pouted pathetically and begged him for mercy, pointing out that she didn't have her checkbook with her. Sean twirled an imaginary moustache and said, "Then you'll just have to find some other means of repaying me, my pretty."

Bree widened her eyes, stifling her laughter. "Why, whatever can you mean, sir? Surely you don't expect me to yield my virtue to you. You couldn't be such a cad."

"Oh, couldn't I?"

In a moment he was around the box that served as a makeshift card table. Bree cowered away from him in mock terror, feeling her heart begin to beat with slow, heavy thuds as she caught the reckless gleam in his eyes. He caught her up in his arms and carried her the few feet to the sleeping bag, the humor leaving his face as he laid her down and knelt beside her. Her arms came up to encircle his neck and his lips met hers, his broad frame blocking out the flickering firelight.

She awoke several hours later, her hand reaching out automatically and then her eyes opening when she encountered empty space. Sean knelt on the hearth, his back to her as he placed more wood on the glowing coals in the fireplace. As the flames licked up around the wood, he half-turned toward her and she noticed again the terrible scar that marked his back. She blinked sleepily as he threw a last branch on the fire and stood up to cross the few feet to the sleeping bag. Bree admired his body, taking pleasure in the rippling muscles just visible in the flickering light.

He crept into the bag beside her, his arm sliding under her head to settle her more comfortably against him. Seeing that she was awake, he tilted up her face to deliver a quick kiss to her mouth before letting his head fall against her soft hair. She rubbed her fingers absently through the hair on his chest, enjoying the rise and fall of the muscled expanse.

"How did you get that scar?"

"Which one?" he asked, stifling a yawn.

"The long one on your back." Her hand slid around his side to touch the mark in question.

"I'd like to be able to say that I got it rescuing some fair maiden, but the sordid truth is, I got it in a fight in a bar in Singapore."

Her brows drew together and she was shocked by the flash of raw jealousy that surged through her. "Was it over a woman?" She thought she had controlled her voice to make it sound like an idle question, but she felt the chuckle that reverberated in his chest.

"No, it was not over a woman. To tell the truth, I don't even remember exactly what started it but it was just a friendly brawl until some idiot pulled a knife." His voice came to an abrupt halt and when he spoke again it was in a very different tone. "If you don't stop that, I'm going to be forced to mete out a severe punishment."

Bree grinned mischievously and let her hand continue its apparently aimless wandering across his taut stomach. The disturbed timbre of his voice pleased her enormously. Her fingers slid lower and, with a groan, Sean grabbed her hand, pinning it next to her head as he rolled over to trap her willing body beneath his aroused frame.

"I warned you." He murmured the husky threat and Bree smiled up at him sensuously.

"I guess I'll just have to take my punishment like a big girl, won't I?"

"I guess so." His mouth captured hers with gentle force.

Eight days after her fall Sean announced that they would leave the next day. He was carefully shredding the last of their dried beef into a pot of soup when he spoke and Bree looked up from her game of solitaire, startled by his abrupt tone.

"Tomorrow morning we'll walk down to the road. It shouldn't take us more than an hour or so to get to it. We can pick up a ride from somebody and you should be home by tomorrow afternoon."

For a moment Bree could only stare at him, at a loss to cope with the surge of conflicting feelings that his announcement brought out. They couldn't stay here forever, she knew that. She didn't even want to stay here forever. Of course, she was anxious to get back and reassure her family that she was safe. And she wasn't exactly averse to the idea of hot showers and real food, but the past few days in this ramshackle cabin had been the closest to heaven she had ever come and she was afraid to leave it behind. *Don't be foolish,* she scolded herself. *Your happiness doesn't depend on a rundown hut in the middle of the Rockies!* No, but it did depend rather frighteningly on the man who knelt in front of the fire and she was suddenly acutely aware of the fact that he had made no mention of any future together for them.

At her continued silence Sean glanced over at her. Her face held a bewildered, frightened look, and with a soft oath he dropped the last of the jerky into the pot and set down his knife before getting to his feet and moving over to where she sat on the sleeping bag.

"What's the matter, honey? Don't you want to go home?"

"I—I . . . of course, I do. It's just that I've gotten used to it being just the two of us and it's a little scary to think of having to deal with a lot of other people again." She paused and then burst out, "Couldn't we stay here just a little while longer?"

"You know that's not possible. We're almost out of food and the weather can't possibly hold up much longer. It's already past due for a good snowfall."

"I know, I know. It was a silly idea. I just wish . . ." She trailed off without finishing the thought, turning her head away from him to stare into the fireplace. Sean watched her with a tender expression. "I can think of something to take your mind off tomorrow."

"What?" she asked without any real interest. Nothing could wipe out the feeling of dread that was invading her.

His hand cupped the back of her neck, turning her toward him. His dark eyes ran over her face in a look of blatant sexuality that made Bree's breath almost stop. "It

95

seems to me that what you need is something to distract you," he murmured huskily.

"I do?" Her voice seemed to be caught in her throat and she had to force the sound out.

"Hmmm." He bent and traced the outline of her lips with the tip of his tongue and Bree felt her insides melt. "And I know just what to do."

Hours later she could only agree that he had known just what to do to distract her. In the past when he had made love to her, it had been with a tender care that made her feel fragile and precious. She had thought that nothing could possibly give her more pleasure than she already had. Tonight he proved her wrong. Tonight he made love to her with a singlemindedness that at times bordered on a frenzied urgency. His tongue explored every inch of her writhing body until she begged him for mercy. When he ignored her pleas she moved to return his caresses, wanting to drive him as crazy as he was driving her, but he would have none of it. Her wrists were caught and shackled in one fist, and her arms were pinned over her head with gentle but implacable strength while he devoted his attention to her taut breasts. Her head twisted frantically against the down sleeping bag as his free hand began a thorough exploration of her body that left her limp with pleasure.

Time passed without meaning as he taught her things about her body that she had never known. Her hands were released but she was too dazed by the sensations rioting through her to do more than bury them in his hair to pull him closer to her. All the while he kissed and caressed her, he kept up a husky monologue, telling her how much he wanted her, how beautiful she was, and that she had been built for him to love.

The firelight flickered over them, bronzing his muscular body and her own softer shape. The light glistened on his sweat-soaked back as he knelt over her, using all the skill gained in a lifetime of casual encounters to bring pleasure to the one woman he had ever loved. He sternly controlled his own passion and watched her with an almost analytical detachment, intent on driving all thoughts of tomorrow, or the future, or any other man, out of her head. He might never see her again after they returned to civilization, but he would make sure that on this one level at least, she would never forget him.

When he finally gave in to her pleading little cries and covered her slender frame with his own much broader one, Bree's skin glistened with sweat and she greeted his taking of her with a cry of pleasure. Her nails raked his back, leaving marks that neither of them noticed in the heat of the moment. She almost fought him for the embrace, her hips moving to meet his every thrust with a savagery that would have surprised her at another time. Now was not the time for gentle kisses and soft words, and their tongues met and twisted together with the same erotic intensity that characterized their embrace. At the very peak of her pleasure Bree's nails bit into his hips and her eyes flew open to meet the hooded darkness of his. His muffled groan echoed her own soft cry and his body arched above her to give her the very gift of life itself.

Words would have been an intrusion after what they had just shared, and neither of them spoke. Bree watched through hazy eyes as Sean got up to put more wood on the dwindling fire. The pot of soup still sat on the hearth but food held no interest and he barely glanced at it before moving back to lay beside her and pull the sleeping bag shut around them. Bree cuddled up against him, her head falling into its accustomed resting place on his shoulder. Within minutes the sound of her soft, even breathing told him that she was asleep.

Rest did not come so easily to the man at her side. He lay on his back beside her, his eyes wide open and staring at the ceiling, but he was not really seeing the dancing shadows cast by the firelight. His gaze was turned inward and he faced the fact that his life was going to seem terribly empty from now on. With a sigh he closed his eyes and rested his cheek against her tousled hair. Just before sleep came to give his weary mind rest, he murmured three words that she would never hear him say when she was awake.

"I love you."

CHAPTER EIGHT

Bree awoke reluctantly, an inner awareness telling her that she didn't want to face the day, but the sound of Sean throwing more wood on the fire banished the lingering remnants of sleep and she opened her eyes to see him bending over her. Her lips parted to accept his soft kiss of greeting.

"Good morning, sleepyhead. I thought you were going to sleep the day away. Crawl out of your cocoon and I might let you have some of last night's soup."

He waited until he saw that her eyes were really open before moving back to the fire to poke at the embers until they licked up around the new wood. Bree sat up slowly, reaching for the heavy flannel shirt he had given her as the chill air hit her bare shoulders. The little fireplace did a gallant job, but it couldn't quite keep up with the numerous cracks in the walls through which the cold mountain air seeped. She glanced over at Sean and noted that he was wearing just his jeans and wondered that he didn't seem to feel the cold. When he turned his back to her she could not stifle a gasp as she took in the faint red welts that crisscrossed the tanned skin.

He turned at the sound. "What's wrong?"

"Your back. It must hurt terribly." She sounded conscience-stricken and he gave her a broad grin.

"It was worth it." In spite of herself she blushed at the knowing look he sent her and Sean chuckled. "Don't look

99

so guilty. To tell the truth, I can't even tell they're there."
She appreciated his attempt to reassure, her, but she
couldn't really believe him and she was grateful when he
put on his shirt so that she didn't have to look at the marks
she had left on his back.

It seemed to take no time at all for them to eat breakfast
and pack their few belongings in Sean's pack. They used
the last of his toothpaste and she commented laughingly
that they'd better hope they got back to civilization today.
Sean grinned, but the smile did not quite reach his eyes.

She guessed that it was somewhere around mid-morn-
ing when he hoisted the pack onto his back and took a last
sweeping glance around the cabin. The fire had been carefully doused and he had gathered several armfuls of dry
wood and stacked them near the hearth, tucking a pack
of waterproof matches into the stack. If someone reached
the cabin in need of warmth, they would be able to start
a fire quickly and easily.

Bree refused to turn and look at the tumbledown little
building once they left it. Looking back was bad luck.
They took a different path from the one they had been
traveling when she fell. Then, they had been avoiding the
road, but now Sean led them almost directly down the
mountain, wanting to reach the road as quickly as possible. Mindful of her recent injuries, he set an easy pace and
though she knew she was capable of walking faster, she
made no effort to hurry him. Neither of them spoke, each
wrapped in their own thoughts. From the bleak look on
his face, whatever his thoughts were they weren't pleasant.

She looked up in surprise when he drew her to a halt.
In front of them lay a broad strip of black pavement. They
had reached the two-lane road that ran up the canyon.

"If we start walking down the road, there's bound to be

a car along pretty soon." His flat tone made her look at him, but his face was shuttered, revealing nothing of his inner thoughts.

An hour and a half later they were both comfortably ensconced in a small room at the Fort Collins police department and Bree was finding it difficult to adjust to her rapid change of circumstances. Sean's prediction that a car would come along soon had proven true. What they hadn't expected was for it to be a police car. Bree had been surprised at first by the officer's wary attitude toward them, but after thinking about it she realized just how disreputable the two of them must look, her with a rifle slung over her shoulder and Sean with a pistol strapped to his hip. Their attitudes underwent a miraculous change when she identified herself, and within minutes they were seated in the back of the police car though the senior officer had requested that they remove their weapons.

It was only when they were traveling down the canyon listening to the officer call in a report that it had occurred to Bree that perhaps Sean was not as pleased as she was to be picked up by law officers. She had looked at him anxiously but he hadn't appeared to be unduly perturbed and he gave his name easily when asked, so she relaxed cautiously. After almost two weeks of traveling at a speed no faster than a quick walk, she found the sight of the scenery whizzing by disconcerting. A glance at the speedometer told her that they were well within the speed limit, but she still had to restrain the urge to clutch at the door. She listened to Sean converse with the officers, feeling reassured by his easy manner. If he were a criminal of some kind, surely he wouldn't be so comfortable now, would he?

Bree was finding the adjustment to civilization more

101

difficult than she would have expected. After all, she had been on two-week hiking trips before. This shouldn't have been any different, but it was. Maybe it was because they had been so totally cut off from the rest of the world. No one had known where they were and they had had only themselves to rely on. She felt as if she and Sean had been alone for years instead of just days.

The police couldn't have been more polite and helpful. When they arrived at the station in Fort Collins, she and Sean had been fed a hot meal and she had to admit that real food tasted good. The police had found Sean's car almost a week ago. They hadn't connected it to the kidnaping, but they had been keeping an eye on the vehicle, concerned about the possibly lost owner. With winter closing in, they had planned to start a search within a day or two.

Bree found that her father had reacted much as she had expected when approached with the ransom demand. The terrorist who had confronted him with it had been thrown in jail and an all-out search had started for any clues to her whereabouts. She felt a twinge of guilt for the worry her family must have suffered. Not that she could have done anything to alleviate it, but she had been so absorbed in her growing relationship with Sean that she hadn't given as much thought to them as she should have.

The police had more than a few questions of their own and Bree let Sean answer most of them, speaking only to fill in any details he didn't know. No one seemed overly upset over the news that he had killed one of the kidnapers. A team was dispatched to go up the canyon and see if they could recover the body. For a moment Bree thought that Sean was going to offer to go with them, and she clutched at his arm, suddenly afraid to be left alone.

He glanced at her in surprise and saw the nervous tension she couldn't hide. He relaxed back into his seat, giving her hand a reassuring pat. She smiled at him sheepishly, feeling foolish but still grateful that he was there.

After what seemed like hours of answering questions, the officers left them alone, assuring them that her family had been notified and that someone would be arriving any minute to take her home.

"Dare I say 'alone at last'?" Bree asked.

He smiled at her mild humor, but the smile did not reach his eyes. He got to his feet and moved restlessly across the little room to stare at a poster advertising the benefits to be gained from adult-education classes. Bree bit her lip as she studied the taut lines of his back. Something was obviously bothering him. He had withdrawn from her from the moment the patrolmen had picked them up in the canyon. She tried to stifle the disturbing thought that perhaps he was anxious to get her off his hands now that they were back in civilization. She hadn't just imagined the emotional closeness that had developed between them. He had felt more than just sexual desire for her. She was sure of it. She stared at the floor between her feet, feeling the knot in her stomach grow to alarming proportions.

They both looked up as the door opened and a tall, fair-haired man stepped into the room. Sean had only a moment to assess the newcomer's classic good looks before Bree was on her feet with a joyous cry of "Mark!" and had run into the man's arms, open wide to receive her.

Sean turned, feeling the muscles of his neck tighten angrily as Bree was lifted clear off her feet by the intruder. He buried his face in her hair and Sean had to fight the urge to tear him away from her and bury his fist in the man's face. It wasn't as if he hadn't known of his existence, he reminded himself. God knows Bree had mentioned his name often enough.

Mark took hold of her shoulders and held her in front of him to look at her. She brushed the back of her hand across the tears on her cheeks and smiled self-consciously. "You don't have to tell me that I'm a mess. I already know it."

His mouth tilted up in a teasing smile. "You're a mess," he mocked tenderly. His eyes shifted past her to the big man in the middle of the room. He stood braced, legs apart and balanced on the balls of his feet as though ready for a fight. Mark's smile died as his blue eyes met the dark brown of the older man's and he read the implacable hostility there.

Bree suddenly remembered that they weren't alone and she took Mark's hand, pulling him forward until they stood in front of Sean. "Mark, this is Sean Mallory. He saved my life several times while we were in the mountains. Sean, this is Mark."

Mark held out his hand with a friendly smile and Sean glanced down at it as if it were a rattlesnake poised to strike. For a moment Mark thought he was going to refuse to take his hand and he felt a flush of anger surge into his face, but then Sean reluctantly took the outstretched hand, shaking it as briefly as possible. Bree looked from one man to the other, sensing the hostility but at a loss to understand its source.

Mark broke into the building silence before it could become uncomfortable. "I really appreciate your taking care of my little sister. We've—" He broke off as Sean's head snapped up and he stared at him incredulously.

"Your sister!" He turned a fierce look on Bree. "Is he the only Mark you know?"

"Yes. Why?" She was completely bewildered by his strange attitude.

"Why didn't you tell me that Mark was your brother?" he demanded angrily.

"It never occurred to me that you didn't know," she told him truthfully, feeling a tentative warmth uncurl inside her as she realized that he must have thought that Mark was a boyfriend and surely his reaction showed that he had been more than a little jealous.

Mark's brows drew together in a faint frown as he took in not only Sean's possessive attitude toward his sister but her acceptance of his right to be possessive. No one knew better than he how fiercely independent his sister could be. He looked at the two of them closely and what he saw made his frown deepen. Bree looked well, though thinner, but amazingly well considering what she had been through. Her clothes were ratty, torn, and dirty, and the man's shirt that she wore hung past her hips, making her look like an orphan. The man was clean shaven, but that did nothing to enhance his respectability in Mark's eyes. This man was tough, he decided without hesitation. Whatever he had done with his life had left its mark etched in his face. Mark glanced at Bree's face again and what he saw there made his frown become a scowl. Damn! Why couldn't she have fallen in love with someone suitable? The man not only looked like a hard-bitten criminal, but he was too old for her too.

"Let's get out of here. Dad's waiting at home to see you, Bree." He took her arm and pulled her toward the door, breaking into her silent communication with Sean. "You'll come with us, I hope, Mallory," he added reluctantly. "I'm sure my father will want to thank you himself."

Sean hesitated, as if about to refuse, but Bree grabbed his hand, giving him no chance to do so. "Of course he's coming. You don't want to let me out of your sight until I'm safely home, do you?"

With a faint shrug he acquiesced and bent to pick up his pack from its resting place near the door. His pistol was stored safely inside the pack and the rifle that Bree had taken from the terrorist was being left with the police. They were going to see if they could trace it, but they had warned them not to expect much.

The grassy area outside the station was filled with people and Mark muttered an inaudible curse when he saw them. "Reporters! I had hoped to get you home before they discovered you'd been found. I should have known better."

Growing up as the daughter of a diplomat, Bree had become somewhat accustomed to members of the press, but previously her father had always been the target of their interest and she had been on the periphery. This time, however, all their attention was centered on her and she felt like a mouse surrounded by hungry cats as she stepped out of the police station. Mark and Sean closed protectively in on either side of her and two officers moved ahead of them to clear a path through the crowd, but even that was not enough to shield her completely. Microphones seemed to appear from out of midair and questions were shouted at her until she was almost deafened by the noise.

To the more persistent in the crowd, her brother said that she had no comment at this time but nobody paid any attention to him. By the time they got through to the big Cadillac, Bree felt as if she had been wading through mud and she collapsed gratefully onto the wide leather seat.

Sean slid in next to her and Mark made his way around the car and got behind the wheel. With the heavy doors shut, the noise outside faded to a distant rumble.

Brother and sister talked rapidly for the first half hour or so, exchanging news of the past two weeks. Sean sat silent, speaking only when necessary, letting himself relax for the first time since Bree had stumbled into his camp. Some vacation this had turned out to be, he thought wryly. He had gone to the mountains to get away from the constant pressure of responsibility and had found himself not only responsible for Bree but committing the ultimate folly of falling in love with her.

The past two weeks had been physically and emotionally draining for Bree and, despite the rest she had had for the last few days, she found the smooth ride of the car was soon putting her to sleep. She fought it but the intervals between her questions was growing wider and wider and she finally gave up the battle and let herself drift off. Her head fell naturally onto Sean's shoulder and he glanced down at her, his rugged features softening in a tender smile as he slid his arm around her back to pull her into a more comfortable position.

When he looked up his eyes met those of her brother and the unaccustomed softness faded from his face. Mark glanced at the natural way Bree rested against the other man and the possessive position of his arm around her, and he didn't like what he saw. There was more than a trace of hostility in his eyes when they met Sean's deliberately blank expression, but neither man spoke. The remainder of the drive to Denver was accomplished in silence.

The scene outside the senator's red brick house made the one at the police station look like a small family gathering. The lawn was completely covered with reporters and camera crews. The police escort that had helped to clear a path for them earlier was missing and even Mark was somewhat daunted by the prospect of forcing a way through the horde of people. Bree, newly awakened and still groggy, had to fight the urge to suggest that they just stay in the car until everyone went away, even if that took several days.

Mark got out first and worked his way around to the passenger door to meet his sister and her companion. She winced at the sheer volume of noise that poured in when Sean opened the door and helped her out. Once again the two men positioned themselves on either side of her and began working a path through the press of humanity that lay between them and the house. Over and over again Mark shouted that he would have a statement for them as soon as possible, but his promise fell on deaf ears. The click of shutters and the whir of movie cameras added to the overall din and Bree began to feel as though she were being smothered in noise. She shrank back against Sean as one particularly persistent man shoved a microphone in her face and demanded to know if she had been sexually assaulted by the terrorists.

With an angry snarl Sean shoved the man out of the way and bent to scoop her up in his arms. Cameras clicked furiously as he held her protectively against his chest, and using his not inconsiderable size as an advantage, began to push a path through the crowd. Bree buried her face against his chest and let him worry about getting her to the house. Mark muttered a curse under his breath as he followed in their wake, well able to imagine the kind of speculation the other man's action was going to lead to.

The front door opened as they stepped onto the porch

and they hurried inside, shutting the thick door behind them. Sean set Bree on her feet and she barely had time to turn around before her father's arms encircled her in a crushing hug.

"Oh, Dad!" She threw her arms around him and pressed her face against him. For the first time since she had been kidnaped she felt tears fill her eyes and she blinked furiously to hold them back. Her father patted her awkwardly on the back and murmured her name over and over again, his soft voice thick with emotion.

After a moment the senator gripped her shoulders and pushed her away from him until he could look at her. Bree brushed a hand over her dusty, ragged blue jeans, suddenly aware of her bedraggled appearance. "God, I look awful."

James Douglas grinned at her, his handsome, middle-aged face creasing attractively as he looked down at his daughter. The thick dark red hair now sprinkled with gray made their relationship apparent.

"I guess you must be all right if you're already worried about how you look," he teased huskily and she grinned at him.

"It's just that I'm aware of your exalted status. I'm not sure it's even legal to appear in front of a senator looking like a ridge-runner."

This was obviously an old joke between them and he gave her a suitably haughty look. "I'll let it go this time, but if it happens again, I'll be forced to have you arrested." His smile faded and he gave her an intent look. "Are you really all right, honey? When the police called they said you were fine, but I'd just like to hear it from you. They didn't hurt you?"

Bree tucked her arm through his and smiled up at him.

"I'm just fine. They didn't have a chance to hurt me and I'm none the worse for wear."

A stifled snort interrupted her and she suddenly remembered that she and her father were not alone. "Oh, good Lord! How could I be so rude!" She reached out to grasp Sean's hand, drawing him forward. "Dad, I want you to meet the man who saved my life on several occasions. This is—"

"Sean!" Her father interrupted her, stretching out his hand to grasp the other man's. "Sean Mallory! The police said that there was someone with Bree but they didn't mention any names and I certainly never thought of you. What an incredible coincidence! What are you doing in Colorado? The last I heard you were somewhere in South America."

Bree and Mark watched in stunned surprise as the two men shook hands and exchanged greetings. There was a camaraderie between the two of them that made it apparent that they were more than casual acquaintances and Bree's dark brows drew together in an abrupt scowl.

"You didn't tell me that you knew my father!" she interrupted accusingly.

Not in the least discomposed by her accusation, Sean raised one dark brow as he looked at her and his mouth tilted in an indulgent smile. "Didn't I?"

"You know perfectly well that you didn't!"

"How careless of me. I guess it just slipped my mind."

She ground her teeth with irritation, knowing full well that that was all the explanation she was going to get, and not in the least satisfied with it. Her father stepped in tactfully and Bree reluctantly dropped the subject but only temporarily, she promised herself, and Sean grinned at her, well aware of her frustration. Angry, she looked at him as she spoke. "Well, if you all don't mind, I think I'll go wash and change out of these clothes."

"Don't be too long now. Martha has killed the proverbial fatted calf in your honor, honey. And I know you must be hungry." James threw his arm across his daughter's shoulders and pulled her close, as if he couldn't quite bear to let her away from his side, and Bree leaned her head against his shoulder, smelling the inevitable pipe tobacco scent that had clung to his blue wool sweater. That scent, more than any other single thing, made her feel as if she were really home at last. She gave him a peck on the cheek and left the room.

About twenty minutes later, after having sponge-bathed and wearing a caftan, Bree entered the big library. Spread out on a low table in front of the fireplace was enough food to have fed an army. Bree laughed and crossed the room to hug the tall, spare housekeeper. Martha had been a member of the Douglas household for ten years. She had been hired shortly after Bree's mother died and she had been a surrogate mother to the adolescent girl. Her rather austere exterior concealed a heart of pure butter and she hugged Bree now with a strength that threatened to crack several ribs before releasing her. She muttered some comment about checking something in the kitchen and left quickly, an audible sniff the only sign of emotion that was permitted to escape.

James smiled. "Poor Martha. She hates to show any signs of weakness. Sit down, both of you. Can I get you a drink?"

Bree shook her head but Sean requested a Scotch. Bree nibbled at the huge array of food, letting the warmth and security of being home seep into her bones. She put an assortment of food on a plate and moved over to sit on the sofa next to Sean.

"This is my favorite food in the whole world," she told him, closing her eyes, the better to savor it.

"What is it?" he asked suspiciously as she held a triangular wedge of food in front of him. He took a bite with feigned reluctance, chewing it consideringly before pronouncing it as edible.

"Edible! I'll have you know that that is a secret recipe for a shrimp and bacon quiche that chefs have been known to beg on bended knee for."

He grinned, one dark brow arching above his smiling eyes. "Quiche! Don't you know that I need more than quiche to satisfy me?" His big hand caught hers and he brought it to his mouth to take another bite of quiche, ignoring her mock indignation as he met her laughing eyes.

The casual intimacy of the exchange had not gone unnoticed by her family. James Douglas, returning with the drinks, paused, his brows raised in surprise as he looked at his daughter and the man beside her. When he moved forward again there was a thoughtful expression on his face.

Her brother also watched the playful exchange and he scowled darkly. He shot to his feet, causing Bree to look up, startled by his abrupt movement. "I'd better go tell the reporters something before they tear the house down."

The senator nodded. "Good idea, Mark. Just give them the bare bones of the story and tell them we'll give them more when we can. Oh, and keep Sean's name out of it. I'm sure he'd rather not be dragged in if it can be avoided." He glanced at the other man questioningly, and Sean nodded.

"I'd appreciate that."

Mark's scowl deepened, but he nodded shortly before stalking out of the room.

It was early evening before all the questions had been asked. Bree felt as if her voice were going to give out. She did her best to gloss over the entire incident. There was no sense in worrying her father now that it was all over, so she tried to minimize her injuries. Her father continued to look concerned until Sean reassured him that she really hadn't been badly injured. Bree didn't know whether she should be grateful for his intervention or irritated that all it took was a word from him to set her father's mind at ease.

Sean got to his feet and stretched. "I'd better be going. I could use a hot bath and I imagine you could too." He smiled down at her as he spoke and Bree couldn't deny that even though she had cleaned herself up somewhat the thought of a long hot soak with plenty of soap was tempting. She was not sure however that she wanted to let him out of her sight. He had seemed to change from the moment they were rescued and she felt as if he were deliberately putting distance between them. It frightened her.

James was quick to invite him to stay with them, but Sean refused politely. "A friend of mine loaned me his apartment for as long as I wanted and I left some things there before I went camping. I'm getting a little tired of my current wardrobe, what's left of it," he said with a significant look at Bree.

Mark had been silent most of the afternoon but he spoke up now, though not to urge the visitor to stay. "If you want to avoid the news people, you'd better go out through the back. There's bound to be a few reporters still hanging around out front. You'll need transportation. I could give you a ride if you'd like." His eagerness to assist Sean's departure was embarrassingly apparent. His father looked faintly surprised, and his sister glared at him, but the object of his helpful endeavors merely looked amused and refused the offer of a ride.

"If the patrol cars are still out front, I can probably catch a ride with one of them. I don't think they'd mind giving me a lift."

"Let me go make the arrangements for you." Again it was Mark who volunteered to help and the amusement deepened in Sean's eyes.

In just a few minutes Mark returned with the information that one of the officers would pull his car around to the back and he'd be happy to give Sean a lift home.

"Thanks, Mark. I appreciate the help," Sean told him with every sign of sincerity.

Mark ground his teeth in irritation. "Let me show you the way," he said abruptly.

"That's all right, Mark. I think you've been helpful enough."

Bree's tone left him in no doubt as to just what she thought of his helpfulness, but he didn't look apologetic. In fact, his expression became even more grim as he watched her slip her hand through the other man's arm to lead him from the room.

"She's a grown woman now, son. You can't choose her friends for her and she's going to resent it if you try." The senator calmly met his son's blazing eyes, their color so like his sister's, and continued to tamp tobacco into his pipe.

"You're not going to tell me that you approve of him?" he exploded.

"It's not my business to approve or disapprove, but if

114

you want my opinion, I'd say that she could do worse. He's a good man."

"He's too old for her!"

"I don't see that that has any relevance."

Both men turned to face Bree, who stood in the doorway. Mark flushed guiltily at being caught discussing her but he stood his ground.

"He's too old for you and you know it! And besides, he looks like a hoodlum."

"There's more to age than chronological years, Mark. And you might not look quite so respectable yourself after spending two weeks in the mountains dodging terrorists. I happen to be in love with him and I'm warning you now, if you try to interfere in any way, I'll never forgive you." Her quiet determination was more effective than any tirade and his eyes dropped from hers.

"I won't interfere but I don't have to like it," he muttered.

"No one asked you to like it." She looked at her father and the stern expression faded into one of affection. "I think I'll go take a bath and get some sleep. Oh, thanks, Dad, for having some of my clothes brought here."

"Well, honey, when we got word that you'd been found I sent someone to your apartment to pick them up and Martha rushed around to get your old bedroom ready. I just hope you sleep well and I'm just so happy you're finally home."

"Me, too, Dad. I'll see you both later." She nodded in Mark's direction and left the room.

Several hours later she sat up in bed and fluffed her pillow for the fourth time in the last hour. She lay back down and stared at the ceiling. She was tired. Her body craved sleep but her restless thoughts refused to be still long enough for her to get to sleep. Her first evening at home had been pleasant. Mark had refrained from making any more critical remarks about Sean though he did have a tendency to frown at any mention of his name. She had enjoyed being back in the bosom of her family, but she had missed Sean's large presence even more than she had expected to.

Her smooth forehead puckered in a frown. He had been so withdrawn when he said good-bye. She had the feeling that if she hadn't specifically asked him when she would see him again, he wouldn't have gotten in touch with her at all. She tried to shake off the thought. Of course he would get in touch. He might not be madly in love with her but they had certainly shared something that was more than purely physical. He would call her, she was sure of that. She let her eyes drift shut, clinging to the thought. He *had* to call.

CHAPTER NINE

Over the next six weeks Bree found her uncertainty growing rather than easing. Sean's withdrawal, which had started when they were rescued, showed no signs of changing. He kept in touch, however. In fact, she saw him two or three times every week, but he was distant, acting as if she were just a casual friend or, worse still, as if she were the daughter of an old friend. His withdrawal was more than just mental—it was physical too. He rarely touched her and, when he did, it was only in the most casual of ways, a hand under her arm to guide her, a touch on her shoulder to get her attention. And if she reached out to touch him, he politely, casually, and firmly withdrew from her touch.

She was at a loss to explain his change in attitude, unless he really felt nothing more than physical attraction for her and was now trying to get out of the relationship as politely as he could. She would have been in complete despair if it hadn't been for an incident that indicated that he was not as indifferent to her as he would have her believe. It occurred about three days after their return. She had decided that she wanted to move back to her apartment, though her father and Mark had both urged her to stay in their home. She suspected that Mark's concern was not wholly because he enjoyed her company. He hadn't said anything to her, but she knew his disapproval of Sean had not abated and he probably felt that it would be more difficult for the relationship to flourish if she stayed in her father's house. On this point Bree was inclined to agree, but her response was the opposite of his. She moved home.

Sean had called her the day before to see how she was and to let her know that the highway patrol had taken him back up to get his car, which was none the worse for its prolonged rest. The body of the terrorist he had killed had been found, but so far there were no leads to the others. The first snowfall had begun as he was driving down out of the canyon, so it was a good thing they had been rescued when they had. When he showed signs of saying good-bye without making arrangements for them to meet, Bree quickly suggested that he come to lunch at her apartment. He hesitated and she added that she would appreciate the ride across town if he would pick her up and that she knew it sounded silly but she was a little nervous about going back there and it would be nice to have him along. That clinched it and he agreed to come get her in the morning.

They stopped at a market near her apartment to pick up a few groceries since her father had had all the perishables in her refrigerator thrown away. He had also had the locks changed on her front door and she inserted the shiny new key hesitantly. When she pushed open the door she found that her fib had been true after all. She was a little nervous about going back to the scene of her kidnaping and she was grateful for Sean's reassuring presence. Once inside, she relaxed and was able to show him around, though she didn't linger in the bedroom. Her father had sent Martha over to tidy the place up and there was no outward sign of the events that had taken place here two weeks before, but her mind's eye still saw it as it had been when she left, her nightstand drawer open, the blankets thrown back, and her gun on the bed where the terrorists had tossed it.

She shivered as she glanced around the room and commented brightly that she had better get lunch started.

Sean was in the living room examining her book collection and Bree was in the kitchen cleaning mushrooms when she heard a key jiggling in the front lock, and trying to turn it. She dropped the soft brush she had been using and grabbed at a towel to dry her hands. She heard Sean cross the living room and pull open the door.

"Who the hell are you?" Sean's harshly rapped question was answered by another, softer voice.

"I might ask the same of you, but I won't because it's none of my business. Where's Bree?"

Bree stepped into the living room on the heels of the question, taking in the situation at a glance. Sean stood in front of the door, his body braced as if for a fight, his dark eyes narrowed, his whole attitude bristling with hostility. In front of him stood a man who was his complete opposite in complexion. Almost six feet tall but of a slim, whipcord build with sun-bleached fair hair and lazy blue eyes, Brandt Rogers stood comfortably relaxed, his whole appearance suggestive of an indolent beach bum. Bree knew him better than that. He was one of the best photographers in the country and at thirty-five he earned more than a comfortable amount of money in his chosen profession despite his continued insistence that he was too lazy to work.

"Brandt!" She flew across the room to him, feeling his arms close around her for a brief fierce hug before he stepped back to look at her.

"I knew I should have taken you with me to Oregon. How could you get kidnaped when I wasn't around to take pictures of the whole thing! I don't suppose you managed to take along your equipment, did you?" he asked hopefully, and she laughed.

"Well, I tried, but I'm afraid they weren't real keen on having their pictures taken."

"Oh, well," he sighed with regret. "It would have made a great layout." He glanced over her shoulder. "Who's your friend? Maybe you should reassure him that I'm not hostile."

Bree turned, startled to find that Sean had moved to stand right behind her. "Don't tell me that this is another brother that you forgot to mention?" he asked silkily, his narrow gaze still on Brandt.

Good heavens! He's jealous, she thought incredulously and could have laughed aloud at the sheer pleasure of the thought.

"Sean, this is Brandt Rogers, a friend and fellow photographer. Brandt, this is Sean Mallory. He rescued me from the terrorists and saved my life on several occasions."

"Glad to meet you." Brandt held out his hand and Sean took it after an almost imperceptible hesitation.

After a moment Brandt turned to Bree and she could see the amusement that lurked in his eyes. "Since you're busy now, sweetheart, I'll drop by later and pick up a new key. Glad to have you back." He dropped a kiss on her forehead and with a nod to Sean and a brief "Mallory," he was gone.

The silence he left behind was almost audible and Bree risked only a brief glance at Sean's stern face before she slipped around him and went into the kitchen.

She was sautéing the mushrooms to go with the steaks when he came into the room behind her. Her back was to him, but the tingling sensation in her neck told her that he was watching her. She said nothing, waiting for him to break the silence. She hadn't long to wait.

"Do you give keys to your apartment to all your friends?" He spoke abruptly.

"No, just Brandt." She waited for him to ask why he had one, but he said nothing, and after a brief hesitation she went on. It was nice to know that he cared enough to be jealous, but she had no desire to encourage such an unnecessary emotion. "I have a key to his place too. With both of us being photographers, one or the other of us is gone most of the time, so we pick up mail and water plants for each other. We also occasionally borrow equipment or chemicals. Since he lives just upstairs it works out nicely for both of us."

He didn't comment, but she thought she detected a slight easing of tension. His apparent jealousy was something she hugged to herself but it was scant comfort considering that a wall of aloofness still existed between them.

To complicate the situation was her growing certainty that she was pregnant. She was elated by the thought of carrying her lover's child but she was fearful too. How would he react when she told him? Would he think that she was trying to trap him? He must know her better than that!

She knew so little about him. She didn't have any way to judge his reaction to news like that. What he did when he wasn't with her was still a complete mystery. He never mentioned his activities and she didn't have the courage to question him.

Her father had been surprisingly uncooperative too. When she had asked him how he knew Sean he had smiled vaguely and said that Sean had done some work for him once or twice. When she persisted and demanded to know

121

what kind of work, he had looked shocked and told her that she knew better than to ask him to discuss government business. This conversation left her both frustrated and reassured. Frustrated because she really knew no more than she had before but reassured because if Sean had been a criminal, her father would not have been so accepting of him.

Her publishers told her to take as much time as she needed to recover from her ordeal and her bank balance was healthy enough that she could take a month or two off, but Bree preferred to get back to work. She needed something to occupy her thoughts besides wondering about her relationship with Sean and, in the back of her mind was the thought that she might need some financial padding in the near future. She spent hours in the local parks, photographing children at play for an article that was coming up in a magazine for new parents. She developed the pictures in her tiny darkroom, a converted closet, and as the scenes began to take form she could not help but think that someday soon she would have a child of her own.

Reporters were a real problem for the first two or three weeks after she moved back to her apartment. They turned up on her doorstep constantly, at all hours of the day, and a few even rang her doorbell late at night, determined to catch her at home. By telling herself over and over again, sometimes through clenched teeth, that they had a job to do, she managed to be polite. She gave them a brief, edited story of the kidnaping, one that she had outlined with her father and brother. She never mentioned Sean's name and, by some minor miracle, nobody managed to discover it. After telling her story she allowed them to take one or two pictures if they wanted and then

—politely but firmly—she showed them out. After a couple of weeks other items took precedence and her newsworthiness evaporated, leaving her in welcome peace.

In fact, life settled back to normal so rapidly that she sometimes wondered if she had dreamed the whole thing. If it hadn't been for Sean's continued presence and her growing certainty about her condition, the entire incident might never have happened for all the outward impact it had made on her life.

Six weeks after their return to civilization she made an appointment with her doctor. She wanted to be absolutely certain that she was pregnant before mentioning it to Sean. She hadn't seen him in over a week and she was almost positive that he was avoiding her. Pride suggested that if he didn't want her then she certainly didn't need him, but her common sense and love for him decided the issue. He had a right to know that she was carrying his child.

With her doctor's confirmation in hand and an entire platoon of butterflies fluttering in her stomach, she dialed his number and asked him to dinner. He hesitated and she held her breath, sure that he was going to make some excuse for not accepting, but if that was what he intended, he changed his mind and rather abruptly asked what time he should be there.

Her hand was shaking when she set the phone down and she wiped her palms against the seat of her jeans, trying to rid them of that clammy feeling. Her entire future depended on this dinner tonight. His reaction to her news would determine the course of their relationship. She crossed her fingers in a childish gesture of good luck.

CHAPTER TEN

Sean paced restlessly back and forth between the bookshelf and wall until Bree could stand it no more. "If you don't stop walking back and forth like a target in a shooting gallery, I'm going to hit you with something."

She settled herself more comfortably into a corner of the sofa and took another sip of white wine, watching him as he came to an abrupt halt and turned to look at her. No hint of a smile lightened the somber darkness of his face and she felt the knot of anxiety that sat in her stomach expand. Maybe tonight was not a good time to tell him her news.

So far, on the surface at least, the evening had been remarkable only for its blandness. The dinner had turned out well and he had eaten everything she put on his plate, but she had the feeling that he was not really tasting what he was eating. Talk had been desultory, and the only subjects either of them brought up were completely impersonal. The silences had been protracted but not necessarily uncomfortable. It was obvious that he had something on his mind, but her own overriding concerns prevented her from speculating much on what it might be. She had refused his offer of assistance with the dishes, telling him truthfully that it would be easier for her to put them in the dishwasher herself, and he had taken her suggestion that he put some music on and have a drink while she did the cleaning up. Now, as she met his eyes, it was obvious that he had come to some decision that he was not entirely comfortable with and she had a strong suspicion that she was not going to like whatever he was about to tell her.

"I'm leaving in the morning," he said abruptly, biting off the words as if he didn't like the taste of them.

Bree felt the force of his statement like a blow to her chest and she fought to keep her expression blank. She swallowed the rest of her wine in a gulp and set the slim goblet down on the glass-topped end table. She was vaguely pleased to see that her hand was steady. "When will you be back?" she managed to ask calmly.

"I'm not planning on coming back, Bree." He spoke gently but nothing could soften the words and she closed her eyes to hide the searing pain that darkened them to indigo. Sean watched the color drain from her face, leaving her an ashen white and he turned to look at a small print on the wall, not seeing its delicate colors, but unable to bear the sight of her pain. He was doing this for her own good, he reminded himself, but the thought echoed hollowly.

"This . . ." Her voice shook and she paused to regain control. "This is rather sudden, isn't it?" He didn't answer and she went on. "I'm in love with you, you know," she told him with stark honesty, feeling that she had nothing left to lose.

His shoulders tensed as if from a blow. "Don't!" he muttered hoarsely, turning to look at her. "You're not in love with me. You're in love with some knight in shining armor who doesn't exist. You don't know me! You don't even know what I do for a living, for God's sake!"

"So tell me!" she challenged him. "I don't care what you do for a living, but if it will make you feel better, tell me!"

He hesitated momentarily. "I'm a mercenary!" He spit the words out with a mixture of anger and defiance that might have made her smile at a less critical moment. Sheer relief made her want to laugh. After all the possibilities that had gone through her mind, this was nothing.

"Why?"

"Why what?"

"Why did you become a mercenary?"

His brows drew together and he looked at her as if suspecting some kind of a trap. Seeing only interest, he answered cautiously. "It pays well." He waited to see disgust in her face. She continued to look at him calmly and he went on. "After my mother died it was difficult to earn enough to support my brothers. I had no training of any kind and no money to get any. I went into the marines because it seemed like the only thing open to me. Richard was eighteen then and he worked after school. Between the two of us we made enough to keep body and soul together. I discovered that military life suited me and after my stint in the marines a friend of mine got in touch with me and asked if I'd be interested in staying in the same line of work. The pay was good and I took it. I made enough to put Richard and David both through school, so it served its purpose. Once they were on their own, I suppose I could have quit but I didn't know any other kind of life, so I stayed on."

"Is that why you haven't seen your brothers in all these years, because of your profession?" she asked slowly, feeling her way toward understanding.

His mouth twisted ruefully. "Well, it was a little awkward when I dropped in to visit. It's not exactly comfortable to say to your friends, This is my brother, the mercenary. Neither of them ever said anything, but I

126

know it must have been difficult for them to explain me to their friends, so I just quit going around."

"Don't you think maybe you were selling them a little short? It seems to me that they would have been proud to claim you. After all, it's not many young men who would take on the responsibility for two younger brothers. Don't you think you should have given them a chance to express their opinions before you just opted out of their lives?"

"Maybe," he said shortly. "But it was my decision."

"If finding out that you are a mercenary is supposed to make me quit loving you, I'm afraid it didn't work. I had already considered that as a possibility, along with a lot of other much less respectable ones. I even thought you might be a hit man for the mob. I can't say that I would have found that easy to accept, but it wouldn't have changed my feelings for you."

"You don't even know me!" he told her again. "How could you know me?"

Bree got to her feet and looked at him, her face pale but calm. "You're wrong. I know you a lot better than you think. You're stubborn and independent. You're brave but you're not foolhardy. You have a sense of humor and you manage to retain it no matter what happens. You like to think of yourself as being very tough and self-sufficient, but underneath the façade you're a warm human being who needs to be loved just as much as any other mortal. You've got a strong sense of responsibility. You're a very sensual man. You're intelligent, interesting to talk to, devastatingly sexy, and I love you!"

"I'm also forty-three years old, too old for you," he told her roughly.

Her face softened and she moved forward to place one

slim hand against his chest, her silk caftan rustling around her legs.

"Is that what all this is about?" She smiled tenderly and stepped closer, enveloping him in the delicate scent of her perfume. "Sean, what difference does it make? I love *you*, not some number that says how old you are. We could have a good life together; I know we could."

He looked down into her earnest expression and wondered what he had ever done to deserve such torture. She was offering him heaven on a plate and he dared not accept. She might love him now but how would she feel in ten years time when he was a middle-aged man of fifty-three and she was still a young woman? He closed his eyes against the temptation she represented and stepped away from her abruptly. He had to end this now or he'd never find the strength to leave her.

"Aren't you forgetting something?" He made his voice deliberately harsh. "There's more to be considered than just your feelings." He saw her stiffen and forced himself to continue. "I'm sorry, but I just don't love you," he said flatly.

Bree stared at him blindly for a moment and he fought the urge to take her in his arms and tell her he didn't mean it, that he loved her more than he could bear. She struggled to gather together the tattered remnants of her pride and her lips twisted in a bitter travesty of a smile before she turned away from him. "How silly of me. I never thought of that." She picked up a delicate figurine and stared at it as if she had never seen it before. "Perhaps it's just as well that you're leaving. I'd hate to think that I might make a fool of myself again.

"Where will you be going? No, don't tell me. I think I'd rather not know." She paused and he saw her fingers clench violently around the little ornament until he was sure it would break from the pressure, but the glass was stronger than it looked and a moment later she squared her shoulders and set it down before turning to look at him. "I don't suppose you'd like to spend the night just for old times' sake?" Her voice was light, but he could hear the heartbreak in it.

"Bree, I . . ." He shook his head slowly, at a loss as to what to say, but she was already answering her own question.

"No, of course you wouldn't. You must have a lot to do if you're leaving in the morning." She could feel the frozen calm that had enveloped her begin to thaw and she was suddenly desperate for him to leave before she fell apart. "Well, don't let me keep you. Thanks again for all you've done for me. Have a safe trip and take care of yourself. I don't mean to rush you, but I'd really like to be alone for a while."

Sean picked up his coat and turned to look at her once more. He ached to be able to ease her pain, but what could he say? He moved toward the door with the feeling that he was leaving behind the only source of warmth and happiness that he would ever know.

"Watch out for kidnap victims next time you go camping." She had intended to speak lightly, but the memory of the time she had spent with him in the mountains strained her control to the limits. Her voice broke on the last word and she spun away from him, fighting for control.

Sean took an involuntary step toward her, his hand lifting to reach out. "Bree . . . Bree, I . . ."

"Just go. I'll be fine. Really I will. But I would appreciate it if you would leave now."

129

His hand dropped and he stared at her rigid back for a moment, absorbing every detail of her. It was going to have to last him a lifetime. "Good-bye, Bree. Take care."

She held herself rigid until she heard the soft click of the latch as the door closed behind him. She never knew how long she stood there just staring at the row of books in front of her, not really seeing them, her mind a blank. The sound of a door slamming in the apartment next door brought her back to life and she bent stiffly, like an old woman, to pick up Sean's untouched glass of wine and her empty goblet. Moving carefully, as if the slightest jar might shatter her into a thousand pieces, she went into the kitchen and washed and dried the goblets with meticulous care, as if her life depended on their being perfectly clean and spot-free.

That done, she looked around, wondering what to do now. She went back to the living room and sat down on the sofa. Funny, she had thought that once he was gone she would fall apart and yet now she didn't seem able to feel anything at all. It must be shock, she decided without interest. A glance at the clock showed that it was still early. Less than an hour ago they had just finished dinner.

Her hand moved to press gently against her still flat stomach. The baby. Thank God, she hadn't mentioned it to him before he told her he was leaving. With his sense of responsibility he would probably have asked her to marry him and she would have done so blindly, sure that he loved her as much as she loved him. She was suddenly achingly glad that she was pregnant. It wasn't going to be easy raising a child on her own, but she wanted this baby desperately. It would be living, breathing proof that Sean had existed in her life. And it would give her something to cling to during the lonely time ahead.

"Looks like it's going to be just you and me, kid," she murmured aloud.

The doorbell rang and she got to her feet with a sudden flare of hope that died almost before it was born. She knew Sean wouldn't be back. Maybe whoever it was would go away if she just didn't answer. She didn't feel like making polite conversation right now. A second demanding ring dashed that hope. Whoever it was, they didn't sound like they were going to go away. With a sigh she smoothed her hand over her caftan and moved toward the door. Maybe they had the wrong address.

"Who is it?"

"Bree? Bree, it's Brandt. Are you all right?"

With a resigned sigh she unfastened the lock and opened the door, stepping back to let him in. "Of course I'm all right. Why shouldn't I be?" She managed what she hoped was a natural smile, her eyes sliding away from the concerned blue of his. "Actually, I was just thinking about going to bed early. Was there something special you wanted?" She led the way into the living room as she spoke and began to fluff the cushions on the sofa.

Brandt watched her for a moment, noting the pallor in her cheeks and the wounded look in her eyes. There was something here that he was not quite sure of and he chose his words with care.

"I was under the impression that you were the one in need of something." She turned to look at him, her brows raised in silent query. "Your large and heretofore hostile boyfriend just called me." She flinched and turned away from his too observant eyes. "He seemed to think that you might need a friend to keep you company tonight."

Bree's fingers dug deeply into the small throw pillow she held and she felt the ice around her heart begin to melt

131

with frightening rapidity. If Sean had called Brandt to come sit with her, it was the final proof, if she had needed it, that he really didn't love her. If he had been even the slightest bit in love with her, he could never have asked another man to comfort her.

She struggled to form a smile as she looked at her friend. "I don't know why he should think that. Why should I be upset because he's leaving in the morning? After all, I don't have any claim on him. It's not as if we were married or engaged or anything."

Uncertain of his ground, Brandt proceeded with caution. "I guess you shouldn't care at all except that I had gotten the impression that you were in love with him. Was I wrong?"

"Oh, Brandt!" His name was a wail of pain, a cry for help, and he opened his arms automatically, lifting her up in them as she threw herself against him. He sat down on the sofa, cradling her across his lap while she cried as if her heart were breaking. He could only hold her while the storm of tears shook her slender frame. He was normally the most peaceloving of men, but Bree was one of his closest friends and, seeing her torn apart like this, he felt a sudden murderous urge toward the one who had hurt her.

Bree cried until she could no longer find the breath to sob and then she lay against Brandt's chest, unable to summon up the energy to move. The soothing stroke of his hand through her tousled hair gradually lulled her into unconsciousness and he gave a relieved sigh when he realized that she was asleep. Moving slowly so as not to disturb her, he got to his feet with her in his arms and carried her into her bedroom, slipping her under the covers of the bed. She obviously couldn't be left alone tonight.

Two hours later he entered the room again to find her still sleeping. Half an hour spent trying to accommodate his six-foot frame on a five-and-a-half-foot couch had convinced him that if he was going to get any sleep tonight, he was going to have to find someplace else to do it. He thought longingly of his own bed waiting upstairs, but he didn't want to leave Bree alone. That left one alternative. Moving quietly, he slipped one of the pillows off the bed and picked up a spare blanket that lay folded at the foot of it. The living room floor might not be the most comfortable place to sleep, but he'd slept in worse.

It was almost two in the morning when Brandt awoke with a start, not sure why he had awakened. He got to his feet and padded softly into the bedroom, feeling a need to make sure that Bree was all right. The room was empty. With nightmare visions of razor blades and sleeping pills running through his mind, he ran into the bathroom, half-expecting to find Bree slumped on the floor in a coma. The small room was mercifully empty and he relaxed fractionally. He went back into the living room, shivering as the cool air hit his sleep-warmed chest. He wished now that he'd thought of grabbing his shirt when he had gotten up. He cursed briefly as he hit his shin on the coffee table and made his way more carefully across the room. The door swung open beneath his hand with a faint squeak and he walked into the kitchen.

The only light on was the one over the built-in stove and it took him a moment to find Bree. She was sitting at the kitchen table, barely within the circle of light. Her hands were cupped around a mug of what his nose told him was cocoa. She had been staring unseeingly at the table in front of her, but, at his entrance, she looked up and gave him a strained smile.

"I hope I didn't wake you." Her voice was husky and rough from her earlier storm of weeping and even in the dim light he could see the ravages pain had wrought on her face. He cleared his throat before speaking, automatically using the lowered tones that seemed to come naturally in the early morning hours.

"I was worried when you weren't in the bedroom," he admitted.

"There's some cocoa on the stove. Why don't you pour yourself a cup and have a seat." She tucked her long, quilted robe more tightly around her, pulling her bare feet up beneath the hem. She waited until he was seated across from her before speaking again. "Did you think I'd kill myself?"

He blew on the hot liquid to cool it down and looked across the table at her. Her gaze was fixed on the cup in front of her. "The thought did cross my mind," he told her honestly. "You were pretty upset earlier."

She gave a short crack of laughter that held nothing of amusement. "Upset! That's an understatement. I was a basket case. But I never contemplated suicide."

"You want to talk about it?"

She shrugged. "There's nothing to tell. I love him but he doesn't love me. He's leaving and he doesn't plan on coming back. That's the whole story in a nutshell. Or, at least, that's almost the whole story."

"What's the rest of it?"

She hesitated a moment and then shrugged again. He'd have to know sooner or later. "I'm pregnant," she announced flatly.

Brandt coughed as a swallow of cocoa went down the wrong way. "Did you say you were pregnant?" he choked out.

"Yes." She raised her eyebrows and gave him a smile of genuine amusement.

Brandt turned the cup around in his hands. "Did you tell him about the baby?"

"No. I found out only yesterday. I was going to tell him tonight, but he dropped his bombshell first."

"Don't you think you should have told him anyway? After all, it's his responsibility too."

"How could I tell him? I know Sean. If I told him I was carrying his child, he would insist on marrying me or, at the very least, he'd want to take care of me. That was a fine idea when I thought he loved me, but it would be sheer hell now because he'd be doing it out of a sense of duty. I couldn't bear that." Her voice shook but she regained control almost instantly.

Brandt looked at her with compassion. "Raising a kid by yourself is no picnic," he warned her.

"I know that, but I want this child desperately. I need it to hang on to my sanity."

"Okay, love. I can understand that. I'll make a great adoptive uncle as long as you don't ask me to change diapers."

She smiled at his expression of horror. Whatever his reasons had been, she was grateful to Sean for sending Brandt to her. His support was just what she needed. The time ahead wasn't going to be easy, but she was a survivor. She would make it.

CHAPTER ELEVEN

Brandt was to prove his friendship over and over during the following two weeks. He was between assignments now and, though he automatically took his camera with him wherever he went, he didn't have anything that he had to do. He virtually moved in with Bree, making sure that she ate and slept and that she got out of the apartment. She protested in vain that all she wanted to do was sit at home and mope for a while. He insisted that moping was not what she needed. What she needed was to get out into the fresh air while she still could. Winter had come early to Denver and there had been snow flurries as early as late October. Now, in mid-November, the city was enjoying a respite before the onslaught of really cold weather. The temperature hovered around sixty degrees. Not sunbathing weather, to be sure, but warm enough for a brisk walk in the park near their apartment building.

After that first night Brandt continued to stay with her at night. She didn't try to talk him out of it, finding that the night hours were by far the hardest to get through. She tried to insist that he sleep in her bed and let her take the couch since it was obviously impossible for him to get comfortable there, but he refused, saying that the floor was not that much harder than his bed. It was not at all unusual for him to wake up in the early hours of the morning to find a light on and he would get up and go to the kitchen where she usually had a pot of tea or cocoa on the stove. They would sit in the kitchen and talk for an hour or two until she began to nod, and then he would herd her back to bed.

They discussed some of the difficulties she might encounter in trying to raise a child and continue her career and some possible solutions to those problems. Bree wanted to find a little house somewhere in a quiet neighborhood to raise her child in. She had some money left to her by her mother and she felt that it would be a smart move to invest it in a home for herself and her child. Brandt agreed with her and they spent a lot of time driving around to various neighborhoods, looking for an area that might be suitable.

He had been with her for over a week when she woke up late one night and lay listening to the quiet in the apartment. What would she have done without Brandt these past ten days? He had bullied her and coaxed her and shown her sympathy, and kept her from sinking into self-pity. Her thoughts drifted, inevitably, to Sean. Where was he right now? What was he doing? Did he ever think of her? Why had he called Brandt and asked him to go to her? Did he think she would console herself with the other man? She had often thought that Sean wasn't entirely convinced that her friendship with Brandt was strictly platonic but that had been when she thought that he loved her at least a little.

Visions went round and round in her head until she thought she would go mad if she didn't stop them. She slid out of bed and walked quietly into the living room, stopping beside Brandt's makeshift bed on the floor in front of the sofa. He had brought down his sleeping bag to pad the floor and she had provided him with a blanket, but he had

137

pushed it aside. He was wearing a pair of cotton pajama bottoms but no top. He looked peaceful and comforting.

With a soft whimper of pain, she sank to her knees beside him and ran trembling fingers over his face, feeling the rough shadow of his beard. She put her hands against his bare chest. His skin felt warm and smooth beneath her touch and she bent closer to him, inhaling the warm masculine scent of him, sliding her palms across the muscled surface of his chest. He stirred as her movements disturbed his sleep and his hand came up to grasp her shoulder. With a sigh of need she slid down to lay beside him, needing to feel the warm presence of another human being. Needing him to need her.

She put her lips to his chest to taste his salty skin.

His reaction was instantaneous as his fingers clenched convulsively around the fine bones of her shoulder. She continued her light, teasing caress, blocking her mind to everything but the taste, smell, and touch of him, wanting only to have him blot out her thoughts. His hand slid down her back and then moved upward and his long fingers slipped into her hair to clasp the back of her head and tilt her face up to his. Her lips met his hungrily, her mouth parting to invite the possession of his, her fingers flexing against his chest. The kiss had barely begun when he was dragging his mouth away from hers and leaning his forehead against hers, his breathing ragged.

"Bree?" His voice was thick, still drugged with sleep. "What the hell do you think you're doing?"

She snuggled closer to his now rigid body, her hands sliding around his back to hold him. "Love me, Brandt. Make love to me." She felt the shudder that went through him and his hand, once again on her shoulder, tightened with almost painful force.

138

"No!" The word was a hoarse mutter and he repeated it again, more forcefully. "No!" With a sudden sharp movement he rolled away from her to sit up. In the dim light thrown by the hall light left burning during the night, she could see the muscles in his back knotted with strain as he bent to put his head in his hands. She sat up and reached out to touch him but he flinched away as if from a burning brand.

"Brandt? Brandt, what's wrong? Don't you want me?"

His harsh crack of laughter was more a groan of pain than an expression of amusement. "My God, you aren't that naive. You know damn well that I want you, but I am *not* going to make love to you."

"Why not?" she asked, bewilderment plain in her voice.

"Because you'd regret it." She started to protest, but he overrode her. "And much as I care for you, I'm not going to be a substitute for another man, not even for you."

"But you wouldn't be a substitute!" she protested.

He turned to look at her, his eyes meeting hers. "Can you tell me with absolute honesty that you weren't thinking of Sean before you started this?"

She opened her mouth to deny it and then flushed guiltily as she remembered that she had been thinking of him just moments before she reached out to Brandt, and her eyes dropped away from his.

"I thought so," he said, reading her expression.

"I'm sorry," she muttered. "I don't know what I was doing. I wasn't consciously thinking of him, you know."

"I know. Listen, don't blow it out of proportion. It's perfectly natural that you should reach out for physical contact. Human beings are basically very physical creatures. But we've been good friends for too long to ruin it by doing something we'd both regret. I'm not saying that

I don't find you attractive, and under ordinary circumstances I'd be more than willing to start an affair with you, but you're in no emotional condition to be making decisions like that right now. Now, if you still find my charms irresistible in a few months, we can discuss it again and I'll see if I can work you into my busy schedule."

She managed to smile, as he had meant her to, but she was sure that she would never be able to face him again.

She left Brandt and went back to bed. She doubted if either of them would get any sleep during the remaining few hours of the night. She finally dozed off near dawn and woke early, feeling unrested and edgy.

Brandt was in the kitchen making his early morning pot of coffee, without which he swore he could not survive the day. It took her several minutes to get up the courage to face him after last night's fiasco, and her posture was rigid with strain when she entered the room. Brandt, however, didn't seem to notice anything amiss. When he saw her he greeted her just as he would have at any other time and turned to get out the milk for cocoa, which had become her morning beverage, since coffee had lost its appeal. Within a few minutes she was just as comfortable with him as she had always been and the incident was never mentioned again—not that it was something to be ashamed of, but it was simply over and done with and there was no need to bring it up again.

That night, however, Brandt slept in his own apartment. She hadn't asked him to stay, but she was sure that she wouldn't be able to sleep without him there. To her surprise, she slept deeply and awoke feeling refreshed. She felt a sense of renewal, as if she were starting on a new life, which, in a way, she was, and for the first time since Sean left, she had a quiet sense of pleasure when she thought of the future.

She had yet to tell her father about the baby. She was confident of his support and love but she just hadn't found the right way to explain it to him. He must have been aware of her involvement with Sean, though he had never mentioned it to her. While she had no doubts about his support, she was not so sure about Mark. She had seen almost nothing of him since her return to her apartment and when she had seen him, he had made his disapproval of Sean more than obvious. She didn't think he would actually stop seeing her, but she was fairly sure that he was going to give her a rough time about it.

She had a chance to test out her theory sooner than she had expected. She had finally managed to convince Brandt that she was fine and he had gone out and left her alone when Mark came by. She was surprised to see him on her doorstep, since as far as she knew he was in Washington, D.C. He cut short her greeting.

"Are you alone here?"

Her brows rose at his abrupt tone. "Yes. Why? Were you expecting the F.B.I. or something?"

" 'Or something' is more like it." He followed her into the living room and took a seat on the sofa across from her. "Are you still seeing Mallory?"

Bree studied him in silence for a moment, noting the signs of agitation in her normally calm brother. His suit was rumpled and creased, as if he had slept in it, and his thick blond hair, always immaculately combed, looked as if he had been running his fingers through it, something he would never do.

"As a matter of fact, I'm not seeing him anymore."

"Thank God!"

141

His muttered prayer made her frown. "Would you mind telling me what all this is about?"

He thrust his fingers through his hair, confirming her suspicions as to how it had gotten so tousled. "How much do you know about him, Bree?" Instead of answering her question, he asked another one of his own and she throttled her impatience and answered cautiously.

"I know as much as I need to. Why?"

"While I was in D.C. I asked a friend of mine to find out what he could about the man." His eyes slid away from the sudden anger in hers. "I know you think it's none of my business, but you *are* my sister and I can't help but worry about you. I didn't like him when we met." He ignored her sarcastic, muttered "You're kidding" and went on. "After I found out that he and Dad knew each other, I asked Dad about him but he wouldn't tell me anything. It worried me, so I got this friend to look him up. You won't believe what he found out, Bree."

"I already know what he found out."

"The man's a mercenary! What do you mean, you already know?" he said when her remark sank in. He looked at her incredulously. "How did you find out? Is that why you're not seeing him anymore? Because you found out what he is?"

"I hate to disillusion you, Mark, but that had nothing to do with it."

"You mean you knew he was a common mercenary and you continued to see him?" His horrified disbelief might have been funny if she hadn't been so irritated.

"There is nothing common about Sean. As a matter of fact, I didn't find out about it until the last time I saw him, but it was something I had suspected, along with a lot of other less respectable professions."

"Less respectable! What could possibly be less respectable than being a hired soldier?"

"Well, he could have been a hit man for the mafia."

He stared at her as if he had never seen her before. "Do you mean to sit there and tell me that you suspected him of that and you still went on seeing him?"

"In all your righteous indignation, you seem to be forgetting that he saved my life on several occasions and that if it weren't for him, I might not be alive today. You act like you would rather I were dead than defiled by contact with someone who doesn't measure up to your standards!"

He had the grace to flush beneath her scathing look, but he stuck doggedly to his point. "I'm very grateful for what he did for you, but that doesn't mean I think he's a good person for you to be involved with. Look, I don't want to argue with you about it. I suppose it doesn't matter what he was as long as you're not seeing him anymore."

"What have you got against him? So he's a hired soldier. So what! You fought in Vietnam and I seem to recall that that was a cause that you didn't particularly believe in. Why is it so terrible that he's a mercenary?"

"Let's not argue about it," he pleaded. "He's gone and we can forget him." He started to get up. "Why don't we go out to lunch and just relax together? We used to be able to talk to each other without fighting. Maybe we could figure out how to do it again." He gave her an appealing look and Bree was tempted to just let it slide, but there wasn't going to be an easier time to tell him.

"You'd better sit down, Mark. I've got something to tell you."

He sank back onto the sofa, his expression a mixture of concern and wariness.

"I think you should understand that I'm not seeing

143

Sean anymore, but it was his decision, not mine. I don't care what he was or is, I love him." Mark moved as if to interrupt but she went on. "I'm pregnant."

Her brother slumped back against his seat and stared at her in stunned silence. "His?" he finally managed to croak.

She nodded. "Yes, and before you say it, no that's not the reason he left." His guilty start confirmed that that was what he had been thinking and her mouth quirked in acknowledgment. "Sean doesn't know about the baby. His reasons for leaving had nothing to do with this." She fell silent, waiting for his tirade to break over her head. He would come around eventually, but she knew he was not going to accept it without a fight.

"I assume that you want this child." She nodded and he went on with a faint sigh, worry drawing his brows together. "You realize that it's not going to be easy trying to take care of a child and earn a living at the same time."

"I know that." She could hardly believe that he was taking it so calmly.

"And I don't suppose you'd be willing to let Dad and me support you until the child is ready for school?" His brows rose in query and he gave another sigh when she shook her head. "I didn't think so."

"Are you feeling all right?" she asked.

"Why shouldn't I be all right? I admit that this has been a shock but it's not enough to kill me."

"It's just that . . . Well, this isn't quite the way I expected you to react. I expected more . . ." She trailed off, searching for a tactful way to put it.

"You were expecting me to throw a fit, is that it?" He grinned at her guilty nod and then his expression sobered and he leaned toward her to emphasize what he was about to say. "I did a lot of thinking after you were kidnaped.

There wasn't much else I could do. When I saw that you'd taken your boots, I thought that maybe they had been taking you to the mountains and I knew you had your knife so that you weren't entirely helpless. I spent hours just driving up and down the canyons. I even drove up the one they had taken you to, but, of course, there was nothing to see. I don't know what I was looking for—a big neon sign with your name on it, maybe. I knew the chances of finding you were virtually nil, but I just couldn't stand to sit around doing nothing. So I drove around and did a lot of thinking."

He reached out and took her hand, looking down at it as he continued. "I thought about how we always seemed to argue when we were together and I remembered that it didn't used to be that way. You used to follow me around like a puppy, hanging on every word I said, always willing to get involved in whatever I was doing no matter what it was and we never fought then. It was only when you began to grow up and develop other interests that we started to argue all the time. I realized that I had been jealous when you stopped depending on me and so I tried to dominate you. Only you weren't about to let me get away with that and so we fought.

"It just sort of got to be a habit to try to push you into things and I had gotten so used to it that even when I got over being jealous of your other interests I still had this habit that I wasn't even consciously aware of." His grip on her hand tightened and he raised his head to meet her eyes. "I know I've been hard to get along with for the last five or six years but it was just because I love you so much. I never really thought about it until you were kidnaped and then I realized just how much you meant in my life.

If you could sort of try to overlook what a butt I've been, maybe we could learn to be friends again."

Bree blinked back tears as she met his eyes. "I haven't ever claimed to be perfect myself. You mean an awful lot to me, too, and I don't think it will take all that long to be friends again." She smiled at him and changed the subject, wanting to lighten the atmosphere a little. "Did you say something about lunch a while ago? I'm starving."

Over the next two months Bree came to appreciate her family more than she ever had. Not one word of criticism was ever uttered by either her brother or her father. Both of them did everything they could to make life easier for her. She was fairly certain that her father called in a few favors and pulled some strings to get her photography assignments that were close to home, but when she taxed him with it, he looked hurt and asked her what he had ever done to make her think that he would interfere with her career.

He, as had Mark, offered her financial assistance, but he was not at all surprised when she refused. The only thing he insisted on was that she move into a small house that he owned in a pleasant residential district. The property had been bought as an investment several years before and had been rented out until recently, when the couple who had been living there moved to Arizona. The agent who handled the property had been looking for new tenants but had yet to find anyone suitable. Bree was reluctant to accept it but the location was ideal and the house was exactly what she had been looking for. There was even a small utility room that could be converted to a darkroom with very little effort. She eventually agreed to move in but only if she could continue to pay the rent just like any other tenant.

She felt a pang of regret at leaving her old apartment. She had been there for three years and it had been comfortable. She knew she was going to miss Brandt's company and he had complained plaintively that now he would have to hire a plant sitter when he had to travel. He had promised to visit her and she knew she wouldn't be losing touch with him. Though she refused to admit it even to herself, the thing that bothered her most about leaving her old address was the thought that Sean might come looking for her and find her gone. It did no good to tell herself that he wasn't coming back and that even if he did, she wouldn't be hard to find. Her new phone number would be given to him if he called the old one. She still could not shake the thought.

There were other thoughts that intruded into her peaceful existence. Whenever she turned on a news program and heard reports of fighting in some faraway region of the world, she felt a sick feeling in the pit of her stomach. Was Sean there? Was he still alive or was he lying wounded in some inadequate medical facility?

It got to the point where she couldn't bear to watch the news and yet some inexplicable force inside her insisted that she turn it on every evening. She would sit, with sweaty palms, through the reports of fighting, her heart pounding as if she had just run a marathon.

Would it have been any easier if he had loved her, she asked herself. Would she have felt more secure knowing that he would be coming home to her if he survived? She tried to imagine what it would be like to wait for him to come home, always wondering if this would be the time he wouldn't make it.

She came to the painful conclusion that maybe it was better that he had left as he had. This way she might wonder if he was alive, but she could always imagine that he was. It would have been even more difficult to build a life with him and then to have it all destroyed by a sniper's bullet. She didn't think that she had the strength to live on the cold edge of fear for the rest of her life.

She was too busy to dwell very much on what might have been if Sean had loved her. Between work and learning all there was to learn about being a mother, she didn't have a lot of time to sit and ponder. She was not exactly happy, but her life was full and she was looking forward to holding her child. If her thoughts dwelt on the baby's father more than she would have liked, she told herself that the memories would fade with time.

CHAPTER TWELVE

Bree muttered a curse under her breath as her chilled fingers fumbled, putting the key into the lock. If she didn't get warmed up soon, she was going to freeze into a solid block of ice right on her own doorstep. Then with a sudden click the key slid in and she was able to turn the lock. Her mittened hand struggled briefly with the icy handle before it yielded and she opened the door. She sagged with relief as it shut behind her and she leaned back against the panel, letting the warm air of the little house begin the slow process of thawing out her bones. She tugged the wool cap off her head, shaking loose her hair before tugging at her mittened hand with her teeth. With one hand freed of the cumbersome mitten she quickly stripped the other one off and bent to work at the laces on her boots.

This was the last assignment she was going to take this winter, she told herself. She was getting too awkward to be playing like a mountain goat up and down snowy slopes. She had come very close to taking a nasty fall more times than she cared to remember during the last week and she just wasn't going to risk that again. Maybe she could print some of those pictures she had taken of the children in the park last month and see if there was anything worthwhile among them.

She flexed her stocking feet with a sigh of relief. Those boots might keep her warm but they felt like they weighed at least half a ton apiece. Her warming fingers moved to the buttons of her heavy coat and then froze as some sixth sense alerted her to the fact that she was not alone. She raised her head slowly, not knowing what to expect, one hand moving behind her to grip the doorknob. If necessary, she could be out the door in a matter of seconds. John and Kathy were home next door. She had seen their lights on when she drove up.

Her fingers slid limply from the knob as her eyes focused on the broad figure standing in the doorway to the living room. She had left the living room light on a timer when she left for this assignment and she hadn't bothered to turn on the hall light when she got home, so his figure was seen in silhouette but she had no doubts about who it was. She sagged back against the door as Sean stepped forward.

"How did you get in?" That wasn't what she really wanted to know. She wanted to know what he was doing here at all, but she said the first thing that popped into her head.

"You pick up a lot of useful skills after twenty-three years as a soldier. Here, let me help you with that," he said as she fumbled uncertainly with her coat.

"No!" she said sharply, and he stopped instantly. "I mean, I don't want to take it off just yet. I think I'll wait a little while." She didn't know why he was here but she wasn't going to take off her coat. Its bulky thickness was an adequate shield for her condition. Without it the slight swell of her stomach was more than obvious. "I'll just leave it on until it warms up in here," she finished lamely, moving past him and into the living room, her mind churning with conjecture about his presence.

He followed her, and the room that had always seemed nice and cozy was suddenly much too small. She jumped when his hands came down on her shoulders and twisted indignantly as he stripped the protection of the coat from her. He threw it carelessly on a chair and then his hands grasped her shoulders again, turning her to face him. She stood rigidly in front of him, her hands clenched into tight fists at her sides and her eyes fixed on his chest. The thick creamy wool sweater that had been so warm and heavy this afternoon felt like a mere gossamer veil as his eyes traveled over her to rest on the bulge of her stomach.

"It's plenty warm in here without the coat and I already know about this," he told her, his hand going to touch her belly.

She jerked back from him as if burned.

"Well, good for you. You've convinced me that you're omnipotent," she said acidly. "Now, would you mind telling me what you're doing in my house?" Still, she refused to look at his face, moving restlessly across the room to turn on another light.

"I was waiting for you, obviously. I was beginning to get worried. You shouldn't be out driving when the roads are in this condition."

"Well, it seemed like a much better idea than walking," she pointed out sarcastically. "What are you doing here? And don't tell me that you were waiting for me. That's not what I meant and you know it. I want to know why you were waiting for me. I thought you said good-bye quite thoroughly two and a half months ago. Was there something you forgot to say?"

She stood next to the lamp, her body rigid with tension, her eyes fixed on the neckline of his black sweater, and she saw the movement of his chest as he heaved a sigh, his hand going up to comb through his hair in a familiar gesture that sent a shaft of pain through her.

151

"I know I've got a lot of explanations to make, but do you think we could sit down and maybe have a cup of coffee while I make them? I've spent the last four days traveling and I'm just a bit tired."

She let her gaze touch on his face and she had to admit that he did look exhausted. Dark circles were etched under his eyes and the lines bracketing his mouth seemed more deeply drawn than she remembered. Despite her determination to remain untouched, she softened slightly. "Why don't you sit down and I'll get you some coffee. When was the last time you had a meal?"

He shrugged. "I stopped at a truck stop sometime last night and had a sandwich, but I'm not really hungry."

"Well, I am and you might as well eat with me." She gestured to a cupboard in the corner of the room. "I think there's some Scotch in there that Brandt brought over at Christmas. Why don't you have a drink while I make us some omelets." She ignored the way his mouth tightened at the mention of Brandt and went into the kitchen.

She went mechanically about the business of cracking eggs into a bowl and grating cheese. Thinking of his appetite, she opened a can of mushrooms and chopped some green onions that she found in the bottom of the refrigerator. Her own appetite had disappeared but she had to eat.

What was he doing here? After all these weeks she was finally getting to the point where she didn't think of him every waking minute and dream of him all night. She had begun to accept the fact that she was going to have to make a life for herself and her child without him. Why couldn't he have stayed away? Seeing him was just going to open wounds that had barely begun to heal.

She set water to boil for instant coffee for him and then poured the egg mixture into a skillet. While his omelet was cooking she opened the carton of milk she found in the refrigerator and sniffed it suspiciously. She had meant to throw away all the perishables before she'd left, but there hadn't been time. She shrugged. It smelled okay.

A few minutes later she wiped her damp palms nervously on her hips and forced out a normal voice to tell her uninvited guest to come and eat. In the seconds before he appeared in the narrow doorway, she was struck by the sudden thought that maybe she had imagined his presence, maybe it had all been a hallucination. She wasn't sure whether she was sorry or glad when he dispelled the thought by stepping into her little kitchen.

She gestured to him to sit down and then sat opposite him, picking up her fork and toying with the fluffy omelet.

"I didn't expect you to go to all this work. A cup of coffee would have been just fine."

She shrugged without looking up. "It's no big deal. I had to fix something for myself anyway."

Sean studied her downcast head for a moment before picking up his fork and cutting into his food. They ate in complete silence, Sean with apparent relish, Bree with dogged determination. The last thing she wanted right now was food, but it gave her something to do. She was supremely aware of the man across the table. She finished her omelet and set her fork down with a sharp clatter.

"Would you mind telling me just what you're doing here and how you knew about the baby?" Her voice came out harsh, as if she hadn't used her vocal cords in a long time. She pushed a piece of lint around the edge of her place mat with the tip of her finger and waited for his answer.

He pushed his empty plate aside and leaned his elbows on the table. He had pushed the sleeves of his sweater up his arms almost to the elbow and Bree could not help but notice the thickly corded muscles of his forearms. She dragged her eyes away from him and focused them on the table again. Things would be much easier to cope with if she didn't look at him.

Instead of answering her questions he asked one of his own. "Did you know you were pregnant before I left?"

She hesitated and then answered truthfully. "Yes."

His breath hissed between his teeth and the muscles in his arms bulged as he clenched his hands into fists. "Is it too much to ask why you didn't tell me?" His voice was husky with anger and Bree felt her nervousness evaporate with the heat of her own anger. How dare he take that self-righteous tone with her! She raised her head and met his eyes squarely for the first time, taking a perverse satisfaction in the simmering anger she read there.

"Actually, I intended to tell you about it, but it seemed a little awkward to bring it up after you informed me that you were leaving. I had just found out that day, you know, and I was going to tell you when you came for dinner, but you told me your news first." She had the satisfaction of seeing pain replace the anger in his face.

"Oh, God! I'm sorry, Bree. I had no business demanding any explanations from you."

She hardened her heart against him. "No, you didn't. Now, would you mind telling me why you're back and how you found out about the baby?"

He hesitated, uncharacteristically uncertain. "I have a friend here in Denver who lives near your father. He knew that I was the one who was with you in the mountains. When he found out that you were pregnant he got in touch with me and . . ."

Bree exploded out of her seat and paced across to the

154

counter where she stood with her back to him, gripping the tile with knuckle-whitening force. Sean broke off his explanation and stood up, turning to watch her with wary attention.

"Do you mean to tell me that you've had someone spying on me for the last two and a half months?" she demanded.

"Not spying, exactly, but . . ." She spun to face him, her eyes flashing with rage.

"What would you call it? Has he been giving you full reports of where I go and whom I see? Has he?" Her voice had risen to just under a shout, but she didn't care. She couldn't remember ever experiencing such anger in her life and she was filled with the urge to hurt him as he had hurt her. "Has he reported to you how many times Brandt has spent the night and how many times I've spent the night at his apartment?"

His face whitened and the muscles in his jaw tightened, but she could barely see him through the mingled tears and anger. With a frustrated groan she picked up a cup from the counter and hurled it at the opposite wall, feeling a momentary satisfaction as it shattered into a hundred pieces, followed by her horrified realization of her loss of control. She turned back to the counter, her slender frame shaking with sobs as she bent over it.

When Sean gripped her shoulders and turned her toward him, she tensed briefly against his hold and then relaxed, letting him press her head into the soft wool of his sweater while she cried. When the storm of tears subsided she found herself in the living room, cradled across Sean's lap as he sat on the sofa. She should move, she thought vaguely, but she couldn't summon up the will power to make her muscles obey her. His hand stroked the tangled hair from her forehead and she kept her eyes closed, leaning against him, letting him soothe away the pain.

"You shouldn't have come here," she told him tiredly. "I was just beginning to get used to living without you and now I'll gave to start all over again. You shouldn't have come," she repeated.

"Shh." His breath stirred her hair as he bent to kiss her flushed forehead. "I had to come." His lips moved down to her closed eyelids, tasting the salt of her tears as he traced a path across her cheeks.

Weakly, her head fell back against his arm. She should stop him, she told herself. She couldn't just let him walk back into her life and start kissing her as if nothing had changed. But it's been so long, another, weaker part of her said. Just a little while longer, just a few more minutes of pretending that he loved her, and then she'd stop him.

"Oh, God, Bree. It's been so long," he muttered against her neck, unconsciously echoing her thought. The painful longing in his husky voice was her undoing. With a half sob her hand slid up his chest to his neck and buried itself in the thick hair at the back of his head. Her mouth tilted to meet his and all thoughts of stopping him vanished as his mouth came down on hers.

Her lips parted easily to welcome the thrusting probe of his tongue and she felt rather than heard the groan that rumbled in his chest as he tasted her eager response. He kissed her long and deep, seemingly unable to get enough of her. His left arm supported her back, his hand resting on her hip. His free hand began a slow, rousing explora-tion of her body, sliding up her waist to rest just beneath the full curve of her breast. Bree shivered with the intensi-ty of the sensation and she felt her breast swell to fill his

156

palm as it moved to cup the ripe mound through the thickness of her sweater.

He drew back with a muttered curse and she sat up on his lap to help him strip the offending garment over her head. All thoughts of stopping him were pushed aside. She wanted him as much as he wanted her and his groan of satisfaction found an echo in her sigh as his fingers unhooked her bra and the scrap of fabric was discarded.

Her hands clutched his hair as he bent to touch the rosy peaks with his lips. His tongue rubbed each nipple with gentle violence until it sprang into throbbing life before taking one between his lips to suckle it to pebble hardness.

He drew his head back to survey the results of his actions with satisfaction before looking into her passion-dark eyes. "I didn't mean for this to happen when I came here, but you want it, too, don't you?"

She stared back at him, feeling the rigid tension of his body and seeing the pleading in his face and she knew she had only to say that it wasn't what she wanted and he would let her go, but the words would not come. She loved him. It didn't matter that he didn't love her. It didn't matter that he would probably be gone in the morning, leaving her to pick up the pieces of her life again. She loved him and she wanted him and she could no more send him away from her now than she could cut off her own right arm.

Her smile was half rueful acknowledgment of her own weakness, half love as she leaned against his broad chest and placed a soft kiss at the base of his throat. "Aren't you awfully overdressed?" she asked huskily.

His arms tightened around her until she thought her ribs would crack, and then he was surging to his feet with her in his arms. He strode unerringly toward her bedroom, his eyes never leaving her face as he shouldered the door open and crossed the room to set her on her feet next to the bed. He pulled his own sweater off and began to unbutton his shirt and Bree was touched to see that his fingers were trembling as he worked at the buttons. It took her only a moment to unbutton the waistband of her slacks and step out of them and she moved to turn down the bed.

When she turned back to him he stood before her magnificently naked and she could not help the breath that caught in her throat as she took in his beauty. He had lost weight since she had last seen him and his muscles stood out tautly beneath his smooth skin. She put one hand to her stomach, suddenly self-conscious of her thick-waisted appearance. Would he think she looked ungainly? His reaction banished the worry.

His hands came out to rest on the still gentle swell and his expression in the dim light that spilled in from the hallway was almost reverential. "Beautiful," he murmured. "More beautiful even than I'd remembered."

His hands slid around her back to draw her against him and she gasped as she felt his arousal. Her hands slid up his hair-rough chest, her fingers pausing to tease at the flat nipples. She smiled at his immediate reaction before letting her hands trail up to his shoulders and then on the back of his neck. She stood on tiptoe, arching her thighs into his, and tilted her head up, her mouth warm and inviting as she looked at him from between half-closed lids. "Kiss me, Sean. Love me."

"It's been so long, Bree. So long." The whispered cry of longing was stifled against her mouth. They had been too long apart to take time to drag out their coming together. In a matter of seconds they lay together on her wide bed, arms and legs entwined as each sought to bring the other the greatest possible amount of pleasure.

Sean's mouth slid moistly down her neck, nibbling at the sensitive cord on his way to greater treasure and Bree's hips arched in involuntary response when his teeth bit gently at the swollen curve of her breast, his tongue soothing away the small pain before he repeated the caress. His knee slid between her legs and she whimpered softly as his thigh brushed against her soft skin. He used his teeth and tongue and the hard warmth of his thigh to turn her into a frantic, writhing creature who could only beg breathlessly for him to complete the embrace. Her hands wandered restlessly across his back and shoulders, kneading and caressing the taut muscles, her nails biting into him as her passion increased.

His mouth rose from her trembling flesh to find her lips, and she met his kiss with an almost violent demand of her own. "Now. Please, now." Her words were half pleas, half commands, and with a stifled groan he rose above her, his heat pressing against her soft warmth. His eyes glittered down at her.

"Tell me, Bree. Tell me what you want." His voice was a husky rasp in the dim room and she opened drugged eyes to look up at him, seeing the hard desire in his face but seeing something else, too, a kind of pleading, a need for reassurance.

"I want you. I need you. I love you." She gave him everything he asked for and more, asking nothing in return, needing to banish the unaccustomed uncertainty from his eyes. Her nails bit into his lean hips as she arched to meet him, his groan of completion echoed by her cry as she was filled with him. Beads of sweat broke out across his forehead as he fought to retain his control and love her gently. But Bree didn't want him to be gentle now and the writhing demand of her body beneath him forced him to set a new pace. She almost purred with satisfaction as his frame moved on hers with a need as great as hers. She reveled in the thrust of his hips, her nails raking across his back as his movements tightened the hard knot of tension that had begun to build inside her. With a gasping cry she felt the tension snap, sending her spinning through space at a dizzying speed. Sean's hoarse shout came to her dimly as he shuddered in release.

She was only vaguely aware of him rolling to the side, his arm curling beneath her shoulders to pull her against his lean frame while his other arm sought to untangle the covers and pull them up around the two of them. It had been a long and tiring week, and adding to that the unexpected meeting with Sean and their cataclysmic coupling, it was not surprising that Bree found herself drifting off to sleep almost immediately, her tousled head pillowed on his shoulder, her arm flung across his chest as if to hold him to her.

CHAPTER THIRTEEN

Sean roused slowly. For the first time in months he felt rested and content. His nose twitched as the unmistakable smell of brewing coffee drifted into the room and he opened his eyes to bright sunshine pouring through the muslin curtains that covered the windows. He didn't need to reach out an arm to know that he was alone in the bed; he had known that from the moment he woke. He stretched luxuriously, feeling an easing of the tension that had gripped his muscles ever since he had last seen Bree.

He swung his long legs out of bed and reached out to pick up his clothes. They had been neatly folded and laid on the small chair that sat under the window. God, he must have been dead to the world to have slept through her getting up and moving around. He hadn't slept that heavily in years, but he had to admit to feeling more rested than he had in years. Things were going to be all right, he thought with satisfaction as he strode into the small bathroom that adjoined the bedroom.

A half hour later Bree glanced up from her morning cocoa to see him standing in the kitchen doorway, his hair still damp from his shower. He was wearing fresh jeans and a heavy cream wool sweater that made him look dark and dangerous, and she had to suppress a shiver of excitement as she took in his blatant masculinity. She cleared her throat nervously.

"I see you found your duffel bag." She nodded to his clean clothes and freshly shaven cheeks.

His eyes darkened with irritation as he moved into the room. "You shouldn't have carried it in. I could have gone out and got it this morning."

She shrugged. "I had to go out anyway, and I thought you might like some clean clothes. I was just about to fix myself some breakfast. Are you hungry?"

He considered pursuing the issue of her carrying his duffel bag and then changed his mind. It was already done. "I'm starved, but why don't you sit down and rest while I fix us some breakfast."

"Why should I?"

"Why not? It wouldn't be the first time you've eaten my cooking and you're still alive to talk about it. Besides"— he shifted uncomfortably beneath her skeptical look— "shouldn't you be resting or something?"

Bree could not restrain a delighted laugh as she got to her feet. "The days when pregnant women languish in bed for nine months are gone. I'm in perfectly good health and I'm not in the least bit tired. Besides, it makes me nervous to have someone else in my kitchen, so why don't you sit down and let me fix breakfast. I made a pot of coffee for you. I'm afraid it doesn't appeal to me much these days."

For the next forty-five minutes they talked easily on a variety of impersonal topics. Sean sat back and enjoyed the sight of her moving about the kitchen getting a meal for him. His eyes dwelt frequently on the bulge of her stomach, still slight but visible beneath the soft blue sweater. It gave him an indescribable feeling of pride to know that his child lay nestled inside her.

Bree, for her part, set aside all thoughts of the future and let herself enjoy his presence in her home. She stole

162

glances at him, storing up memories for the time when he would be gone again. They were both putting off the talk they knew had to come, but she didn't care. She just wanted to savor his presence for now.

They ate breakfast in companionable silence and then he insisted on helping her with the dishes. She couldn't help but grin at seeing him up to his elbows in suds. He glanced at her and, catching her expression, raised one heavy brow in silent inquiry, but she just shook her head and he didn't pursue it.

With the dishes cleared away she couldn't think of any more excuses to linger in the kitchen. She went into the living room, acutely aware of him following her. The day was heavily overcast, with the weather report predicting more snow by nightfall, and Bree had left the curtains drawn against the gray skies outside. Now she moved around the room, turning on lights and giving the room a feeling of cheerfulness.

"It's a shame you don't have any wood. It's the right kind of day for a fire." She followed his eyes to the empty fireplace and she had to agree that a fire would be nice.

"There's a big stack of wood on the back porch. Brandt brought it up from the woodpile for me last week, but I haven't been home to use it."

Sean's back stiffened at the mention of the other man, but she was trying to find a crochet hook that had fallen behind the sofa cushions and didn't notice his reaction or departure to get the wood.

A little while later Sean dusted off his hands and looked at the crackling fire with satisfaction before he sat down in a chair across from Bree.

"I didn't know you crocheted."

"I don't. This is not crocheting, it's making a mess, or

so my teacher informs me. I'm supposed to be making a baby blanket, but every time I take it into the store to show it to her, she makes me rip most of it out and start over again. I think I'm giving her an ulcer."

He chuckled at the satisfaction in her tone, but she had the feeling that his mind was not really on what she was saying. They sat in silence for a while and the tension in the room began to build. She searched desperately for some light casual remark to ease the charged atmosphere, but her mind had gone completely blank and she could only sit there, silent, and stare at the mess she was making of the yarn.

"Bree."

She jumped when he spoke, his voice sounding unnaturally loud. She looked at him, surprising a look of uncertainty in his dark eyes.

"Marry me."

She stared at him in total disbelief. "What?"

Now that the words were said, he seemed to have regained his customary assurance. "I want you to marry me." When she made no reply, he went on, leaning toward her as he spoke. "Last night you said you loved me. I—I don't know what your feelings for Brandt Rogers are, and I don't care what your relationship with him has been these past few months." He gritted his teeth as he had forced out the lie. "That's my baby you're carrying and I want to help you care for it. I want to take care of you. I know I'm a lot older than you are, but you said before that it didn't matter. I wouldn't go that far." His mouth twisted in a rueful smile. "But maybe we could work around it. I'm not rich, but if there's one thing to be said for my profession, it's that it pays well. I've got quite a lot of investments and I own my ranch free and clear. If something happened to me, you'd be taken care of." He paused, as if trying to think of something more to persuade her and Bree, recovering from the shock of his proposal, set aside her mangled yarn and leaned forward to touch his tightly clasped hands, bringing his eyes back to her face.

"You don't have to feel this way, you know. I never wanted you to feel obligated to me because of the baby. That's why I didn't tell you about it before you left. I want this baby. It was my choice to keep it and it's my responsibility."

His eyes fell from hers and he turned his hand beneath hers to clasp her fingers in a grip that was almost painful. "The baby isn't the only reason I want to marry you. It just gave me a good excuse to do what I wanted to do all along." His grip tightened and she almost cried out. "I'm in love with you," he said huskily. He ignored her gasp and went on. "I've been in love with you almost since we met."

"Why didn't you tell me?"

"Look at me, Bree! For God's sake, I'm forty-three years old! Fifteen years older than you! And it's not just the age difference. When you were in grade school I was packing a machine gun through the jungles of Southeast Asia. I'm not ashamed of what I've done, but it's been a rough life. I've seen things and done things that you can't even begin to comprehend. I'm old, Bree. Not just in years, but in experience."

She moved to kneel in front of him, her hands gripping his fiercely as she looked into his tortured face. "I don't care what you've been or what you've done. I know you're not a boy, and I know that there were a lot of years that you were already an adult while I was still a child. None

165

of that matters. Don't you see? I love you. I love what you are now."

With a groan he freed his hands and reached down to gather her up into his arms. She met his kiss willingly, her arms going up to encircle his neck, her fingers sliding into his hair to hold him even closer. She could only murmur her approval beneath the bruising pressure of his mouth when he got to his feet with her still in his arms and moved toward the bedroom.

Again she saw him made clumsy with haste and emotion. His fingers fumbled awkwardly with the buttons on the shirt she was wearing beneath her sweater and, with a tender smile, she pushed aside his hands and completed the task herself. Their lovemaking had always been supremely satisfying but today there was an added element to it that made every touch, every whispered word, more meaningful, more intense. They moved together with the grace of ballet dancers, their bodies perfectly in tune to each other's needs, and when they attained the high peak and then fell in a long tumbling dive, Bree thought her heart would stop with sheer ecstasy.

She lay with her head on his shoulder, listening to his breathing gradually slow to a more normal pace and running her fingers through the sweat-dampened hair on his chest, taking idle pleasure in its coarse texture.

"Can Rogers make you feel like that?" His harsh words had barely penetrated into Bree's consciousness before he was continuing. "No! Never mind. I shouldn't have said that. It's none of my business."

She had sat up, holding the sheet to her breast, and now he sat up, too, swinging his legs over the side of the bed and sitting on its edge, presenting her with a view of his back. The muscles in his shoulders were bunched tightly, the skin across his back taut with tension as he leaned forward, his forehead resting against his hand.

"What makes you think I've been having an affair with Brandt?"

"You told me you were. Last night you asked if I knew how many times he'd spent the night, if my 'spy' had told me. I never had anyone spying on you, Bree. My friend lives down the street from your father and he just thought I'd want to know about your pregnancy. I never asked him to spy on you."

"I believe you," she told him soothingly, unable to resist trailing her fingers over the terrible scar on his back. He flinched as if she had touched a new wound, but she ignored the movement. "I have never slept with Brandt, Sean." He turned to face her, surprise and disbelief plain on his face.

"You don't have to lie to me about it. I—I can't say that it's easy for me to accept, but I can cope with it. After the way I left you, I don't have any right to be jealous of anything you did while I was gone."

She met his look with love and absolute honesty. "I'm telling you the truth. Brandt is just a friend, a very dear friend, but still just a friend." She hesitated and then went on. "When you first left I was devastated. Brandt spent a lot of time helping me cope with everything. There—there was an occasion when I wanted or I thought I wanted him to be more than just a friend." She paused, her eyes dropping away from his and her fingers plucking nervously at the sheet. She licked her lips. "Brandt refused. He said that I would end up regretting it and that he was very fond of me but that he was not going to be a substitute for another man, not even for me. I thought he was wrong at the time, but I soon realized that he had been right and that I would have hated myself if he hadn't stopped it when he did."

"Thank you." He reached out and gathered her against his chest. "I know I didn't have any right to be possessive after the way I left, but it was tearing me apart to think of you with him. And in case you're wondering, I haven't touched another woman since I met you. I couldn't have even if I had wanted to. I just couldn't get you out of my mind." He felt the faint easing of tension in her and he drew her closer.

Bree lay against him contentedly, reveling in his closeness. Her senses were filled with him, her nose took in the rich tangy scent of his aftershave, her fingers explored the taut skin of his shoulders and his heart beat with reassuring solidity beneath her ear. She closed her eyes, the better to savor the feeling of warmth and security that surrounded her.

CHAPTER FOURTEEN

It was late evening before she was forced to come face to face with the future. They had spent the day in undemanding pursuits. With more snow predicted, Bree wanted to get some food in the house before the weather worsened. Sean took her shopping and, though she pointed out that she was quite capable of doing it alone, she didn't really argue. She didn't want to let him out of her sight right now.

Grocery shopping with him along was a unique experience. For every practical, sensible item she put in the cart, he added two extravagant, impractical things. When she protested the addition of six jars of very expensive pickled herring, he stated firmly that it was a well-known fact that pregnant women were inclined to strange cravings and that, this way, he wouldn't have to try and find pickled herring at three o'clock in the morning. When she pointed out that she detested pickled herring and was therefore unlikely to get a craving for it, no matter what her condition, he gave her a boyish grin that was so appealing it made her want to weep and told her that if she didn't eat it, he would manage to keep it from going to waste.

She had never seen him in such a teasing mood and this new dimension to his personality made her love him even more, if that were possible. Her brief shopping trip took a lot longer than she had planned and instead of one or two bags of food, the trunk of his Mercedes was completely filled. Sean insisted on paying for everything. When she tried to protest he gave her such a fierce look that she subsided without a word.

It was only after they had shared a candlelight dinner that the tranquility was shattered. The dishes were done and they were sitting in the living room. The curtains were drawn close against the snowy night. The promised snow had arrived just before sundown and had been falling with deceptive gentleness ever since. Sean had built up the fire in the fireplace so that it crackled with cheerful brightness, the only source of light in the room except for one table lamp near the sofa. Bree was curled up on the sofa, her head on his shoulder as she stared into the flames.

He broke the companionable silence with the words she had been dreading all day. "When will you marry me?"

She shut her eyes in brief anguish before withdrawing from his light hold until she sat next to him, still close but separate, and what she had to say was going to widen the gap still farther. Why couldn't he have waited until tomorrow to ask that, or next week, or never?

He sat forward, sensing her disturbance. "Bree? Honey, what's the matter?"

She realized that she couldn't put off this confrontation no matter how much she longed to do so, but she tried anyway. "There's no rush. We can think about it later." She tried to keep her tone light and unconcerned as she got up and moved across to the fireplace. Maybe he would let it drop. Oh, please, let it drop, she prayed. She moved the screen back and tossed an unnecessary piece of wood on the fire, aware with every fiber that he, too, had risen. She turned away from the fire, bracing herself to look natural, and then gave a startled gasp as she found herself practically in his arms. She had forgotten how quietly he could move.

"What's wrong?" His hands still at his sides, he wasn't touching her at all, but she felt surrounded by him and she kept her eyes fastened on the top button of his dark shirt.

"Wrong?" Her voice came out in a squeak and she took a deep, calming breath before continuing. "Nothing's wrong? Why should it be? Did I say any—"

"Bree." His husky tones broke into her babble and she shut up abruptly, feeling her stomach muscles begin to tighten with dread. She wasn't going to be able to put him off. "Look at me." His fingers under her chin reinforced the command and she raised her eyes to meet his. His dark brown gaze searched the bright blue of her eyes relentlessly and she wondered what he saw there. "You don't have some silly idea that I want to marry you only because of the baby, do you? I'm not saying that I don't want my child to have my name, but that's not nearly as important as knowing that you have my name."

She closed her eyes tight against a sudden surge of tears and shook her head. She couldn't bear the tender concern on his face. "It's not that."

"Then what is it? You do plan on marrying me, don't you?" He spoke lightly but she heard the underlying anxiety in his question and she had to fight the urge to say yes.

"I can't." The words barely emerged from her tight throat and she opened tear-drenched eyes to look at him, seeing the spasm of pain that crossed his rugged features before he could suppress it. The hands on her shoulders tightened their grip to a painful degree, and she winced. Immediately, he released her and turned away with a muttered apology. He stood with his back to her for a moment, one hand coming up to grip the tense muscles at the back of his neck.

"Why?" His voice was muffled but the pain and bewilderment came through and she blinked back fresh tears. "You say you love me but you can't marry me. Why?" He turned to look at her, his face tight with anger and hurt.

"It's hard to explain."

"Well, give it a try."

He was deliberately encouraging his anger in order to hold back the hurt. She could understand that but she felt a spurt of irritation at his sarcastic tone. She moved away from the fire to stand near the sofa, one slender hand resting on its curved back as she faced him.

"I told you before you left that your profession didn't matter to me and, at the time, I meant it."

"I make no apology for what I am," he interrupted her.

"I'm not asking you to! If you would just shut up and listen to me, I could try to explain it to you." She paused and then continued more calmly. "While you were gone I discovered what it was like to love someone who's in a dangerous profession. I didn't know where you were, but every time I heard the mention of fighting somewhere in the world I wondered if you were there. I couldn't help wondering if you were alive or dead or bleeding to death somewhere. I can't live like that, Sean. I couldn't take it!" Her voice broke and she clamped her lips tight to suppress a sob.

Sean stood on the opposite side of the sofa, his shoulders tensed and his head thrown back. His expression stayed dark and hostile and Bree despaired of making him understand her feelings. "I won't let you run me, Bree. Nobody dictates my life and I'm not going to try to be something I'm not, even for you."

"You're not listening to me," she cried, exasperated. "I'm not trying to make you change. I love you just as you are, but I can't live my life always wondering if you're dead. I don't have the kind of courage it takes to do that."

"So what you're saying is that you'd rather throw away everything we have because you don't like my profession," he snarled.

"I don't give a damn what your profession is, you fool." She was shouting by now but she didn't care. "I just can't live like that—worrying constantly."

"I could just as easily get killed crossing the street." As her voice rose his grew softer, but the anger was just as strong. "You lack courage, all right, but what you lack even more is the guts to tell me that you're ashamed to admit that you're in love with a common mercenary!"

Her eyes flashed blue fire and her whole body trembled with rage. "Get out of my house! I don't know how I ever thought I could love such a paranoid egomaniac! Get out and I sincerely hope that I never see you again!"

She turned her back to him, afraid that if she looked at him any longer, she wouldn't be able to restrain the urge to hurl something at him.

"I'll leave for now, but I'll be back." He spit the words at her. "That's my baby you're carrying and it belongs to me just as much as you do. You will marry me even if I have to kidnap you and hold you prisoner until you give in. Nobody dictates what I do and you'll just have to learn to accept what I am."

She heard him move into the bedroom and a few seconds later he came out and stalked over to where she stood. His duffel bag was slung over his shoulder and he had put on his heavy coat but left it unbuttoned. He put his hand under her chin, forcing her head up until her eyes met his. She glared at him in silence, fiercely pleased by the anger she read in his dark eyes.

"I'll be back." His voice was little more than a husky growl and his mouth twisted in acknowledgment of the message he read in her eyes. His gaze dropped to her mouth and she read his intention instantly, but there was nowhere to turn. His hand at her chin held her still as his lips captured hers in a brief, bruising kiss. To her fury, when he released her, he smiled at her and patted her on the cheek. "Just a little something to remember me by." He strode to the door while she was still trying to gather her wits together and turned to smile at her again. "Don't miss me too much. Why don't you go buy something to wear for the wedding while I'm gone."

He turned and ducked through the door and the pillow she hurled at him thudded harmlessly against the solid panel. Dimly, she heard the sound of the Mercedes starting up and then the purr of its engine fading off down the street, but she still stood as if frozen, her clenched fists held rigidly at her sides and her angry gaze fixed on the blank door. A log broke in the fireplace, sending up a shower of sparks as it tumbled its load of smaller wood into the embers below, the small crack of sound serving to break Bree out of her trance. She moved stiffly around the sofa and sat down, her eyes focusing on the hissing flames.

What on earth had happened? A half hour ago she and Sean had been sitting here in cozy silence and she had thought that she couldn't ever be any happier. Now he was gone and she was sitting here wondering where to start picking up the pieces. Her anger had evaporated, leaving her feeling old and tired and, though she hated to admit it, uncertain. Had she done the right thing in refusing to marry him? It hadn't been a snap decision. She had spent a lot of time thinking about it both this morning and over the last two months.

She leaned back and closed her eyes. She had thought that it would be better not to see him at all than to see him only to watch him leave again and again, but could anything be worse than the feeling of desolation that she had lived with since November? Was she being a fool to throw away what they had for fear of what might be? But she had to think of more than just herself now. Her hands moved to rest protectively against her stomach. She had to think of what would be best for her child. She had to think. Sean had said he would be back and she didn't want to see him again until she had come to some kind of decision.

She reached out to pull the phone off the little end table, setting it on the cushion next to her and dialing Brandt's number. She listened to it ring with barely controlled impatience and it was only when his voice came on the line, thick and groggy with sleep, that she thought to check the time. It was after midnight. No wonder he had been in bed. Well, it was too late to worry about it now.

"Brandt, this is Bree. No, no, I'm all right. I'm sorry I woke you. I didn't realize how late it was. Listen, do you remember telling me about that friend of yours with a beach house in L.A. that he said you could use? Do you think I could borrow it for a couple of weeks?"

CHAPTER FIFTEEN

Bree leaned back on the redwood lounge chair and focused her eyes on the ocean in front of her. The sun was just beginning to set and the view before her was so beautiful that if she had seen it in a painting, she would have thought that the artist had imagined it. The ocean itself was a deep blue, with big white-capped waves rushing in only to die out to a mere ripple against beige sands. The sky above was a soft rich gold and hanging suspended just above the horizon was one solitary smoke-colored cloud, outlined by the last rays of the dying sun.

She sipped at her hot tea and hugged her warm coat more snugly around her. Last week the temperature had been in the mid-eighties, but, with an unpredictability that she had been told was typical of southern California weather in February, it had dropped into the low sixties this week. She closed her eyes and breathed deeply, drinking in the rich salt-water smell.

Thank goodness Brandt had had the keys to this place. This vacation was exactly what she had needed. After a month of absolute peace she had finally been able to make a decision about her future and she had plane reservations back to Denver in three days.

Bree sighed and got to her feet, grimacing at her increasing clumsiness. With four months of her pregnancy left, she already felt as big as an ox. The doctor she had seen yesterday had assured her that she was doing fine and that there was no reason why she couldn't fly home, but he had warned her to be prepared for a large baby, maybe even twins. He had recommended that she check for the latter possibility with her own doctor. She grinned as she shut the sliding door behind her and moved toward the kitchen. She wondered what Sean would have to say to the idea of twins.

What had he done when he'd found her gone? She paused in fixing her dinner. He wouldn't have been happy. She was grateful to her father for not asking any questions when she had phoned him from the airport to tell him she was going away for a while. He hadn't asked where she was going and she hadn't told him, feeling that if Sean came looking for her, he wouldn't have to lie.

She carried her plate to the kitchen table and sat down. She had enjoyed this month in the mostly warm and sunny southern California climate, but there was no denying that she was anxious to get home, snow and all.

The rain started around nine thirty and she lowered her book for a few minutes to listen to it spatter against the windows. By ten thirty it sounded as if someone had turned on a tap in the skies. The rain was coming down in sheets and she shivered as she began to undress for bed. She was glad she wasn't out in it.

She was just about to crawl under the covers when a thunderous knocking on the front door almost made her jump out of her skin. She moved slowly into the living room of the small beach house and looked at the front door. Who on earth would be on her doorstep at almost eleven o'clock on a stormy night like this? The knocking came again, louder this time, as if whoever was out there was losing patience. She moved a little closer to the door, considering her options. Only a fool would open the door at this time of night. There could be any kind of weirdo in the world out there. On the other hand, it could be somebody who needed help.

A third pounding came, this time accompanied by a voice that settled her dilemma for her. "Bree? Bree, open this damn door before I kick it in!"

"Sean!"

With a gasp she flew to the door and fumbled with the dead bolt for a moment before her shaky fingers mastered it and she could open the door. She had barely turned the knob before he pushed the door open and stepped into the small, tiled foyer. A blast of cold, wet air hit her legs, bare beneath the hem of her short nightshirt, and she quickly closed the door, leaning back against the solid panel to look at him, hardly daring to believe the evidence of her eyes.

She suppressed her first urge to throw herself into his arms. It was obvious that he was in no mood for affectionate greetings. He shrugged off his dark coat, draping it over a coat hook before turning his attention to his shirt, which was also damp. He glanced up, catching her wide-eyed gaze, and his brows snapped together in a scowl.

"I don't suppose you have any towels in this place," he snapped angrily, jerking at the buttons on his shirt.

"I'll . . . I'll get you some." They were the first words she had spoken since he arrived and she had to clear her throat before she could get the sentence out. She crossed the living room to the tiny bathroom and knelt to pull two fresh towels out of a low cupboard.

What was he doing here? How had he found out where she was? Her brain was spinning with conjecture as she pulled herself to her feet and then stepped back, startled to find that he had followed her into the small room. He had taken his shirt off and he now threw it over the shower rod before turning his attention to her.

"Can I have one of those or are you saving them for a rainy day?"

She flushed, suddenly made aware that she had been staring at his broad chest. With a jerky movement she handed him the towels. He began to rub his thick hair dry and Bree watched, itching to reach out and touch him. The bathroom, which had never been overly large, was suddenly suffocatingly small. There was no room to go around him and with a small sigh she leaned back against the counter, letting it take the weight her trembling knees seemed reluctant to support.

He dropped the first towel and picked up the other one, running it swiftly over his chest and shoulders before putting it down. He smoothed through his tousled hair with his fingers and looked over at her with more than a hint of a scowl on his face. Bree gasped at her first sight of him in the bright overhead light. His face had a lean, almost gaunt cast to it, but what caught her attention was the dark blue bruising that surrounded one eye and the scrape mark across one cheekbone.

"What happened to your face?"

To her amazement, a tide of red crept up his face and his eyes shifted away from hers for an instant.

"Never mind my face. I ran into something. I didn't come here to discuss my face and I didn't plan on talking to you in a sardine can either." He glanced at the narrow room with irritation. "Could we go sit down somewhere?"

"All right. Why don't you go see if there's a dry shirt in your duffel bag and I'll set some water on for tea."

Ten minutes later she sat across the kitchen table from him, stirring her tea with quick, nervous movements. He looked devastatingly sexy with his still damp hair falling onto his forehead and a short-sleeve shirt stretched across the breadth of his shoulders.

"Why did you run away?"

Well, nothing like getting to the heart of the matter without delay, she thought.

"I needed some time to think things out without any pressure."

"And did you think things out?"

"Yes," she admitted, "I've done a lot of thinking in the last month."

"Did you come to any conclusions?"

"Yes, I did." But she volunteered no information on what those conclusions might be. Silence reigned in the room for a few minutes before he set down his cup with a quick, irritated gesture.

"Bree . . ."

"Are you hungry?" She was suddenly afraid to hear what he had to say.

"No, thanks, I ate on the plane. Bree . . ."

"How did you manage to get so wet? Did you have to walk from the airport?"

"I rented a car and it broke down about a mile down the highway. I walked the rest of the way. Any more questions?"

She shook her head, her eyes falling away from his face as she traced a finger through some spilled sugar.

Now that he had her silence, he seemed hesitant about what to say. "I've resigned my commission." It came out baldly and it took several seconds for his words to sink in. When they did her head jerked up and she stared at him wide-eyed, expressions of happiness and uncertainty warring in her face. His eyes met hers squarely. "If you're going to marry me, you'd better find out that one of my worst faults is a dislike of being pushed into anything. I guess I got my way too much when I was a boy. I had actually already resigned before I came to you in Denver, but when you told me you wouldn't marry me because of my profession, all my pigheadedness just reared up and I decided that if you loved me, you'd marry me, no matter what. I guess I'm a little touchy about what I've been and I saw your hesitation as a rejection. After I'd had a chance to cool down I realized just how stupid I was being, but it took me another day to swallow my pride and go back— only you were gone."

The bleakness of his tone told her how much that had hurt and with a tender smile she got up and moved around the table to insinuate herself onto his lap. His arms came up to crush her against his chest as he buried his face in her fiery hair. "I was so worried. All I could think of was how stupid I had been and I kept thinking about you trying to drive in the middle of a snowstorm."

She felt the shudder that went through his big frame and she had to blink back sudden tears at his obvious pain. Her hands slid up to clasp his dark head and she tilted her face until her lips found his, silencing his tortured remembrances with a kiss. His mouth devoured hers, telling her without words how much he had missed her and how worried he had been. There were still questions to be asked but they had no real importance besides the need to reassure him of her love.

Sometime later, minutes or hours, neither of them knew or cared, she sat cuddled across his lap, this time in the living room. One small lamp was the only source of light other than the gas fire that flickered in the central free-standing metal fireplace. Sean was comfortably ensconced on the sofa and, though there was plenty of room next to him, Bree was more than content with her current position. His left arm supported her back and his right hand lay with touching possessiveness on the swell of her stomach.

"I was coming back to you, you know." She spoke softly, reluctant to break the gentle silence that had fallen. "I did a lot of thinking about what you said about throwing away everything just because I was afraid, and I decided that I'd rather have you for at least a little while than give you up altogether. I have plane reservations for Friday."

His lips brushed across her forehead in a silent thank-you. "That means a lot to me, but you were right. It wouldn't be any kind of a life for you, and besides, I had grown tired of it all, even before I met you. That's one of the reasons I took that vacation in the mountains. I wanted to think about the future, make some decisions. I figured that up there, all alone in the peace and quiet, I could think things out."

"And, instead, I ran into you and you had to help me." She didn't really sound too apologetic and she felt his lips tilt in a smile.

"Instead, I ran into an irritatingly independent red-haired witch. The last thing in the world I planned on was to fall in love and certainly not with a woman so much younger than me."

Her fingers trailed idly up his arm. "How did you find out I was here?"

"Your friend, Rogers."

She raised her brows in surprise. "Brandt told you? How did you manage that?"

"Brute force!"

"Brute force?" She sat up and looked at him. "What do you mean, brute force? You didn't hurt him, did you?"

"*I* didn't hurt *him?* I'm the one you should be worried about. How do you think I got this black eye?"

She looked at him for a moment and then went off into peals of laughter. Sean did his best to look offended, but her humor was too contagious and his lips twitched traitorously. "What are you laughing about?"

"You probably deserved it. I don't imagine Brandt hit you without provocation."

"Well, no, not exactly," he admitted. "When I got to your house and found you gone, I went to your father's. He said that you had gone away for a while but that he didn't know where. I didn't believe him, but I could hardly choke information out of my future father-in-law. Mark was in Washington on business and had been for the last week so I figured I could rule him out. My last chance was Rogers. It took me a while to call him, only to be told he was on assignment in Europe and couldn't be reached." She gave a little gurgle of laughter and he looked at her sternly. "It wasn't funny at the time. I didn't know where else to look. I kicked my heels for two solid weeks before Rogers got back. I'm afraid my patience was worn a little thin by then and when he told me that I wasn't going to get your address from him, I slugged him. Did you know he had a wicked left?" He paused reminiscently.

"Anyway, it became obvious fairly quickly that we weren't going to get anywhere that way, so we called a truce. He wanted to know why I wanted to get in touch with you. I told him that it was none of his damn business. We went around and around for a while until I finally admitted that I loved you. He seemed to think that was a good enough reason to give me your address. Only by then my eye was swollen almost shut and it had turned every color in the rainbow. I'd have scared you to death popping up on your doorstep looking like I'd been in a train wreck. So I waited until I looked a little less like the wrath of God and hopped a plane for L.A."

"I hope you aren't planning on punching Brandt every time you see him."

"I think we've come to an understanding." He pulled her back against his chest, settling her more securely in his arms. "Now that all that's taken care of, when will you marry me?"

"Whenever you want." She turned her head to kiss the strong column of his throat, feeling his instant response to the caress.

"How about tomorrow. We can fly to Reno and have a nice honeymoon before going home."

"Ummm. Sounds nice." She trailed moist kisses up his throat to his ear, nipping on his earlobe before tracing around it with her tongue. "Where's home?"

"If you don't stop that, I'm not going to be able to remember my name." He gripped her sides and pushed her slightly away before answering her question, trying to ignore the slumberous blue of her eyes and the inviting pout of her lips. "I have the ranch. If it's all right with you, I thought we could settle there after the baby's born. It's within reasonable distance of Denver. There's quite a bit of wildlife on or near the ranch for you to photograph and we can always travel elsewhere when you need something new for your camera. I'll keep the manager on to run things for me and I thought I'd try my hand at writing. I've always wanted to write a science fiction book and this seems like a good time to give it a try. I think you'll like the ranch, honey."

She reached up to smooth out the faint frown lines on his forehead. "It sounds lovely. Why can't we move there right away? Why wait until after the baby's here?"

"The drylands of eastern Colorado are no place for a pregnant woman in the winter. We get snowed in too often and I'm not going to have you that far from a doctor. We can stay in your little house until after he or she is born."

She smiled at him tenderly, sliding her fingers into his thick dark hair. "How many bedrooms does your house have?"

"Four. Why?" He caught one of her hands in his, turning his head to press a kiss into the palm. "Are you planning on having separate bedrooms?"

"No, but I thought the twins might prefer to have a bedroom each."

For a moment he was completely still, and then he turned his head slowly to meet her mischievous smile. There was a stunned expression on his face. "Twins?" he croaked.

"Well, nothing's positive yet," she told him soothingly. "The doctor just thinks it's a possibility."

"Twins," he muttered again, the dazed expression beginning to fade from his dark eyes. His gaze swept over her body, pausing on the length of thigh exposed by the short nightshirt, on the gentle mound of her belly, and then on the taut outlines of her breasts before coming up to meet her eyes. "This calls for a celebration."

"What kind of a celebration?" she asked throatily, feeling the sudden tautness of his thighs beneath her. He didn't answer her with words. Instead, he surged to his feet with her clasped in his arms and strode into the bedroom to let her slide to her feet beside the bed.

Outside, the windblown rain splattered against the window but the two inside didn't notice it. They were intent only on each other. His fingers worked the buttons at the neck of her nightshirt before lifting the garment over her head and tossing it on a chair. He stripped his own shirt off before sliding his hands around her silken back to pull her against his chest. She gave a throaty murmur of pleasure as her nipples grew taut beneath the gentle stimulation.

"I think you should know what a completely ruthless person you're marrying," he murmured against her throat.

"Ummm." Her hands fumbled with his belt buckle.

"I came here tonight fully prepared to kidnap you if necessary."

"Darling, I would have been the most willing victim a kidnaper ever had."

His jeans were kicked aside and in a moment they lay naked on the bed, his hands sweeping over her body as if rediscovering lost territory while his tongue teased her sensitive throat. "You know I'm considering ravishing you. Are you going to scream?"

"No," she gasped as his mouth began a devastating exploration of her breasts. "I don't believe in screaming, remember? Besides, who would rescue me?"

"No one, my love. No one will ever rescue you from me."

And she could only murmur her agreement.

LOOK FOR NEXT MONTH'S
CANDLELIGHT ECSTASY ROMANCES ®:

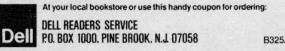

Fans of
JAYNE CASTLE
rejoice—
this is her
biggest
and best
romance
yet!

DOUBLE DEALING

JAYNE CASTLE

From California's glittering gold coast, to the rustic islands of Puget Sound, Jayne Castle's longest, most ambitious novel to date sweeps readers into the corporate world of multimillion dollar real estate schemes—and the very *private* world of executive lovers. Mixing business with pleasure, they make passion *their* bottom line.

384 pages $3.95

Don't forget
Candlelight Ecstasies,
for Jayne Castle's
other romances!

Candlelight
Ecstasy Romances™

$1.95 each

All-new
Candlelight Newsletter

An exceptional, *free* offer awaits readers of Dell's incomparable Candlelight Ecstasy and Supreme Romances.

Subscribe to our all-new CANDLELIGHT NEWSLETTER and you will receive—at absolutely no cost to you—exciting, exclusive information about today's finest romance novels and novelists. You'll be part of a select group to receive sneak previews of upcoming Candlelight Romances, well in advance of publication.

You'll also go behind the scenes to "meet" our Ecstasy and Supreme authors, learning firsthand where they get their ideas and how they made it to the top. News of author appearances and events will be detailed, as well. And contributions from the Candlelight editor will give you the inside scoop on how she makes her decisions about what to publish—and how *you* can try your hand at writing an Ecstasy or Supreme.

You'll find all this and more in Dell's CANDLELIGHT NEWSLETTER. And best of all, *it costs you nothing*. That's right! It's Dell's way of thanking our loyal Candlelight readers and of adding another dimension to your reading enjoyment.

Just fill out the coupon below, return it to us, and look forward to receiving the first of many CANDLELIGHT NEWSLETTERS—overflowing with the kind of excitement that only enhances our romances!

Return to: DELL PUBLISHING CO., INC.   B325E
      Candlelight Newsletter • Publicity Department
      245 East 47 Street • New York, N.Y. 10017

Name_____

Address_____

City_____

State_____ Zip_____